She froze on the shore, unable to move— her gaze locked with his

Damien could see her.

This was what she'd wanted, Olivia reminded herself, as panic choked her. She had wanted him to see her. She needed him to see her in order to exact her revenge.

But when he lifted his arms and reached for her, the panic turned to fear. With dread, she turned to the lake. Every time she went back in, she had to fight harder to reach the surface—to leave those icy depths. But while she'd wanted him to see her, she wasn't ready yet—she wasn't strong enough to face him.

Even now, knowing what he had undoubtedly done to her, she wanted him....

Books by Lisa Childs

Silhouette Nocturne

Haunted #5
Persecuted #14
Damned #22
Immortal Bride #59

LISA CHILDS

has been writing since she could first form sentences. At eleven she won her first writing award and was interviewed by the local newspaper. That story's plot revolved around a kidnapping, probably something she wished on any of her six siblings. A Halloween birthday predestined a life of writing for the Nocturne line. She enjoys the mix of suspense and romance.

Readers can write to Lisa at P.O. Box 139, Marne, Michigan 49435, or visit her at her Web site, www.lisachilds.com.

IMMORTAL
BRIDE
LISA CHILDS

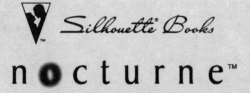

Silhouette Books

nocturne™

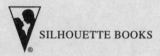

SILHOUETTE BOOKS

ISBN-13: 978-0-373-61806-4
ISBN-10:   0-373-61806-9

Recycling programs
for this product may
not exist in your area.

IMMORTAL BRIDE

Copyright © 2009 by Lisa Childs-Theeuwes

This edition published by arrangement with Harlequin Books S.A.

® and TM are trademarks of Harlequin Books S.A., used under license. Trademarks indicated with ® are registered in the United States Patent and Trademark Office, the Canadian Trade Marks Office and in other countries.

www.silhouettenocturne.com

Printed in U.S.A.

Dear Reader,

I am a voracious reader myself, and my favorite books are romances, of course. I was just eleven when my mom and grandma introduced me to romance novels. I fell as in love as the heroes and heroines in the books I read. I love a good love story—a story of the kind of love that withstands time, that withstands life and death.

Damien Gray, a modern-day warrior, has that kind of love for his immortal bride, but theirs is no simple romance, because one of them is alive and the other is dead—murdered, perhaps at the hand of the man she loves.

I hope you enjoy the story of Damien and Olivia's immortal love.

Happy reading!

Lisa Childs

For my parents, Jack and Mary Lou Childs,
whose amazing love story has spanned sixty years
of marriage. Thank you for your guidance,
love, support and inspiration. Happy Anniversary,
Mom and Dad!

Love,
Lisa

Prologue

Centuries ago…

Crouched on the boulder on the rocky shore, Gray Wolf's image reflected back at him from the moonlit surface of the Lake of Tears. The stripe of white had widened in his black hair, but other than that, he didn't look much older than he'd been before the lake had formed.

Remembering the ravine that water had filled, he winced as he felt again the rocks and branches tearing at his skin as he'd dropped into what his people had believed a bottomless abyss. Yet the rocks and branches had not inflicted the scar that shone faintly on his deeply tanned skin, on his chest, where an arrow had pierced his heart.

He had been dead long before the arrow had killed him, though. The same shaman who'd shot the bow had killed the mother of Gray Wolf's son. But Gray Wolf hadn't known, so he had blamed invaders from a far off land and himself until those invaders returned with *the woman.* Anya—with her hair like moonlight and her eyes like chips of a light blue sky.

The shaman had called her a sorceress, and although he hadn't admitted it, he'd been fearful that she was more powerful than him. So the Wise One had ordered her death as necessary to protect the sacred land of Gray Wolf's people. Only on their land grew the special herbs that could be used in potions that induced supernatural powers. Anxious to redeem himself for what he'd considered his failure to protect his people, Gray Wolf had accepted the mission to kill her.

Instead he had fallen in love with the flaxen haired, pale-skinned beauty. As her touch could bring slain warriors back to life, it had brought him back to life. Twice. First from his self-imposed death due to guilt and remorse and then from genuine death.

She had filled the ravine with her tears, so his body had floated to the surface. She'd dragged him onto this very boulder on which he crouched and had brought him to life again.

And to love. He had never loved another like he loved his Anya. And he never would…

Water splashed as the surface of the lake broke. Arms, as pale as moonlight, glided like ripples through the water, bringing her to him. He gazed down into her light blue eyes, and his once-wounded heart clenched with love. "Anya…"

"My warrior…always protecting me," she said with a wistful sigh.

Even impaled with the arrow, he had saved her from the shaman—throwing her crude dagger and killing the Wise One. Yet Gray could not help but feel the man's spirit lurked, waiting to seek his revenge against Gray Wolf's descendants. But Gray wasn't the *gifted* one. Anya was, as was a female from every other generation of her family. They had no children together—just his son whom she treated like her own. Gray wished for his son, and all his descendants, to find a woman like Gray had, a sorceress, who could save him from the vengeance of the shaman and whose love would create their own Legend of the Lake of Tears.

Chapter 1

She fought her way from the murky depths of the lake, kicking against the skirt of her gown. The wet tatters of material wound around her legs like the tentacles of some monster of the deep, trapping her beneath the icy water. *Help me! Help me!*

She could only utter the words inside her head. Her voice, shaking with fear and desperation, echoed inside her mind. She blinked back the water and tears that blinded her. Faint light guided her toward the surface, yet she could not break free. But she could see the world beyond the lake. She could see *him*.

With the ripples in the water, his face wavered in and out of focus. He crouched atop a boulder on the rocky shore, the wind ruffling his hair, which was all black but for a thin streak of white in the lock falling across his forehead. He leaned out over the lake and tossed long-stemmed roses like stones across the water.

Frantically thrashing her arms and legs, she finally broke free to the surface. But no water splashed. She didn't create so much as a ripple.

His shoulders hunched and head down, he didn't even glance toward her. His face, with sharp cheekbones and deep-set eyes, reflected in the lake. But her face—*none* of her—reflected back from the water. Because *she* no longer existed. He had made certain of that.

"Are the flowers for me?" she asked him through the bitterness and anger choking her.

He lifted his head, as if listening. Then he pushed a slightly shaking hand through his hair, which was long, nearly brushing his broad shoulders. With a heavy sigh, he climbed down from the boulder and walked away, leaving the lake and *her* behind him.

"Damien!" she screamed. But the birds continued to chirp in the trees surrounding the lake, undisturbed by her cry. Because no one could hear her anymore.

But him? He turned back, glancing over his

shoulder at the roses floating across the surface of the water. Did he see her…floating just above? Or did he see only the mist that rolled across the lake every evening as the sun dropped from the sky?

"Damien!" she screamed again, but he whirled away from her and headed up the steep hill to the Victorian house perched on the edge of it. The weathered clapboard and fieldstone facade of the house, with its turrets and gables, blended into the rocky slope—except for its widow's walk, the ornate railing rising eerily above the roofline.

Propelled by anger, she found the strength to pull herself from the lake. She followed him but stopped before the boulder from which he had tossed the roses. A glint of metal drew her attention to a bronze plate affixed to the ancient rock. She reached through the thickening mist and, with a trembling, pale fingertip, traced the engraving in the memorial plate.

Olivia Ann Kingston-Gray, Rest in Peace.

But Olivia could find no peace in death or this limbo in which she existed where her body lay—at the bottom of the Lake of Tears for the past six months. And her restless spirit roamed the rocky shore of the lake, anger feeding off her grief and fear until rage consumed her.

She traced the last words of the inscription. *Beloved*

Wife. Another pretty lie. He had told her so many times—making her trust him, making her fall for him. Olivia didn't know at whom she was more angry—him for telling the lies or herself for being so gullible that she'd believed him. But now, too late, she knew better.

And she knew what she had to do. Olivia had returned from the dead for one reason. Revenge. Against the man who had killed her. Her husband.

Damien Gray stared down at the lake, which stretched out a half mile from the rocky shore in front of the house. Woods of ancient pines surrounded it. He studied the surface of the lake, watching it grow dark as the last trace of daylight faded into dusk.

Wisps of fog drifted across the gray surface like the roses he had strewn onto the water just a short time ago. He braced his palm against the cool, curved glass of the second-story, turret bedroom window and leaned forward, staring intently across the rocky shore to the lake. He narrowed his eyes, trying to peer through the thickening mist. Trying to see *her.*

Had she been there earlier, floating on the surface of the lake like the fog? Or had her faint image only been his mind—and his heart—playing tricks on him again? Hell, everywhere he looked he saw her now. Maybe she was only a figment of his imagination and his *guilt*.

Or she was actually haunting him…?

He blew out a ragged breath of bone-deep weariness and turned away from the window. Maybe if he could close his eyes and *not* see her, he wouldn't see her when he was awake, either. He needed some damn sleep. *Now*. Before insomnia stole whatever was left of his sanity.

But when Damien turned toward the antique sleigh bed, the last thing he thought of was sleeping in it. He thought again—always—of *her*. And their honeymoon…

Olivia had giggled as Damien kicked open the door and carried her across the threshold into the master suite. "You're really pushing this macho thing by carrying me up the stairs," she teased. "You better put me down."

Never. The thought flashed through his mind, and his arms tightened around his new bride.

"Trying to get away from me already?" he asked, keeping his tone light and teasing even though he worried that she was. That she might. Because it had happened before.

Her hand clenched on his shoulder, and she smiled

up into his face, her pale blue eyes shining with love. Or so he'd thought at the time. "I'm right where I want to be," she assured him.

"Good," he said with satisfaction, "because you are not going anywhere."

She lifted her chin and challenged him. "Oh, I'm not?"

"No, I forbid it." And he wasn't entirely joking.

She tilted her head. "Hmmm…as I recall the vows that we spoke today, we agreed to respect each other, but there was no mention of obeying."

"Hmmm…" he mocked her, "I recall you definitely agreeing to obey. Have you forgotten so soon, Wife?"

"Nice try, Husband," she mocked back. "But if you don't let me go, I can't give you your surprise…."

His gut tightened with apprehension. "Surprise?" He hated surprises. He'd had one too damn many.

Taking advantage of having distracted him, Olivia wiggled out of his arms. "Yes, I have a surprise for you." She grabbed a small suitcase from the chest at the foot of the bed and carried it into the bathroom. "I'm glad the bags were brought up."

"Nathan brought them up when we went down to the lake," he said, glancing toward the curved turret windows that overlooked the rocky shore and the

Lake of Tears. But he didn't move toward the window; he could not move farther away from her.

"Nathan?" she asked through a crack in the bathroom door.

"My cousin and the caretaker of the house and lake," he explained—as much as anyone could explain Nathan Gray.

"The shaman?" she asked.

Obviously she had spent enough time in town to hear about Nathan. Usually the residents of the village of Grayson, in the Upper Peninsula of Michigan, were reticent with and suspicious of strangers. But from the moment Olivia had come to town, she had been accepted as if she belonged. And she did—she belonged with him.

"Yes, Nathan is believed to be a shaman," he said. But no matter what the townspeople, or Nathan, thought, Damien struggled to accept the legends and the beliefs of the past as anything more than fairy tales. He was too pragmatic and cynical to believe in the supernatural.

"I want to meet him," she said.

Probably to question him about the lake, as she had persistently questioned Damien since they had first met. Her fascination with the legend of the

Lake of Tears should have forewarned him…of the tragedy to come.

"I want to thank him," Olivia explained, "for bringing up the bags."

Then she stepped out of the bathroom and into the soft light of the crystal chandelier. And for a moment Damien stopped breathing, the air trapped in his lungs, as he stared at his bride. Even though she hadn't worn a wedding dress for their civil ceremony, she had been beautiful in an ivory skirt and jacket, with her hair pinned up. Now she looked bridal—in a white silk-and-lace robe and gossamer gown with her platinum hair shimmering like moonlight around her shoulders.

"I want to thank him, too," Damien said, his voice raspy as desire for his bride overwhelmed him.

Her fingers trembling, she plucked at the long, full skirt of the gown. "It's not too much? I know we wanted to keep things simple." Dark pink color flooded her pale skin. "And it's not like we've never done it before…."

He reached out and pressed a finger across her lips. "Shhh…" He sought to settle her nerves even as ones of his own rushed up to squeeze his chest. "Tonight is our first time."

Beneath his finger her lips curved into a smile of amusement. "Damien…"

"Tonight is our first time as man and wife." He moved his finger back and forth across the silkiness of her full lips. "Tonight is the first time I sleep with my bride…."

"This bride," she murmured, her eyes soft with vulnerability.

Since he'd met her, which had actually been a few short months ago, he had witnessed only her strength and confidence. He had never glimpsed her insecurity until that moment.

Did she have doubts or regrets about marrying him? "Olivia?"

"I'm sorry," she said, shaking her head so that her hair swirled around her shoulders. "I shouldn't have mentioned her—"

But now that she had, the pressure that had weighed on Damien for years returned. He shoved a hand through his hair and said, "Maybe we shouldn't have come here."

"You didn't want to," she reminded him. "I talked you into it."

And he should have followed his gut instinct and stayed away from the lake. Hell, maybe he should have sold the house and property. Unlike Nathan and Olivia, with their fascination with the past, Damien preferred to leave it behind and move on to the future.

But he and Olivia had met here at the lake, and so he had allowed himself to be persuaded to return for their honeymoon.

Their honeymoon.

He was the one who needed to move on, to let the past go and focus on the future. His future with Olivia.

"I intend to give you *everything* you want, Olivia," he promised.

She gazed up at him, her blue eyes soft, and insisted, "I only want you."

He lifted his hand and ran his thumb over the gold band on his finger. "You have me."

"I'm greedy," she said, her lips lifting in a smile again, but one that was more wistful than amused. "I want *all* of you."

He had worried that she would want more from him than he could give. But yet he had proposed. Maybe it was the gambler in him that had compelled him to risk his heart again. Or maybe it was *her*.

"You have all of me," he assured her. "I'm here."

Not at the chain of casinos that usually consumed all his time and energy but that had rewarded him for his hard work and dedication with more money than he would ever be able to spend.

"And I'm with you—*only* you." Because of her, he was able to move on beyond the pain of his past.

He pushed his fingers into her soft hair, cupping her head and tipping up her face so she'd meet his gaze. "You are *everything* to me."

Her breath shuddered out in a warm caress against his throat and chin. "I love you. I *love* you."

Damien, as a gambler, was used to taking risks. But he didn't like to drop his poker face and reveal his hand. Too many times the other person had proved to be bluffing. But this was Olivia, and even though he hadn't known her long, he felt he knew her well, well enough to trust her. "And I love you…."

"Prove it to me," she challenged, shrugging off the white silk robe to leave her creamy shoulders bare but for the narrow straps of the gown. Through the thin lace, he caught glimpses of her body—the swell of her breasts, the shadow of her navel and her rosy areolas. Under his intense stare, her nipples hardened and penetrated the flimsy material.

He groaned. "That's some gown."

"Negligee."

"Whatever it is, I like it," he said as he slid his finger under one of the straps. "But I'd like it even more off you."

"You're the one with too many clothes on," she complained, reaching for his tie, unknotting and then sliding it free of his shirt. Next she attacked the buttons, undoing them to bare his chest to her soft hands and softer lips.

His heart pounded hard beneath her mouth. He tangled his fingers in the silken strands of her hair and tugged gently so that her face tipped up to his. Leaning forward, he pressed his mouth to hers. He nibbled first at her lips then deepened the kiss, sliding his tongue into the sweet warmth of her mouth, as he couldn't wait to bury himself inside her body.

His blood was rushing through his veins as he slid his mouth from hers, over her delicate jaw to her neck. Her pulse pounded with a passion nearly as fierce as his. He moved his hands over the silk and lace covering her body, tracing the dip of her waist, the curve of her hips…

Then he cupped her breasts and rubbed his thumbs across the nipples protruding through the gown. When he replaced one thumb with his mouth, suckling through the lace and tugging gently with his teeth, Olivia moaned and tangled her fingers in his hair, pressing his head against her breasts. "Damien, please…."

He lifted his gaze to meet hers. The pale blue irises nearly swallowed by her enlarged pupils, she stared down at him. "Please," she repeated, "give me *everything*…."

"Oh, I intend to," he promised as he pushed the straps of the gown from her shoulders. The white lace slithered down her body, puddling at her feet, leaving her pale skin bare but for the flush of passion. He lifted her in his arms and carried her to the bed and vowed, "I'm going to give you everything, Wife, and not just tonight…."

But for the rest of their lives. He had intended to spend his life making her happy, not mourning her loss.

That night had marked the beginning of their marriage and was supposed to have been the beginning of their life together. But less than a week later, before the honeymoon had ended, Olivia was dead.

Rubbing a slightly shaking hand over his face, he stared out the window again. A storm had rolled in with his turbulent memories. Dark clouds hung over the fog-enshrouded lake while thunder rumbled in the distance. Then lightning broke the clouds, illuminating the sky, the lake, the rocky shore—and *her.*

Olivia, wearing that same silk-and-lace gown he'd taken off her on their wedding night, walked along the shore. The lightning caught in her hair, making the long blond strands as luminescent as moonlight.

He pounded his fist against the curved glass and screamed her name: "Olivia!"

* * *

Lightning flashed, cutting through the mist to illuminate the rocky shore and the house on the hill above it—and the man standing at the window of the bedroom in the second story of the turret. Thunder drowned out his voice, but from the way he moved his lips, she could tell he screamed *her* name.

She froze on the shore, unable to move, her gaze locked with his. Then the dark clouds dropped closer to the earth, blocking the house and *him* from her vision. But her tension did not ease; she was as restless as the weather. The crisp spring wind whipped around the lake, shaking the boughs of the ancient pines. Thunder boomed with such force that the rocks on the shore beneath her trembled, and above her, the windows of the house rattled.

Then lightning cracked again, illuminating the house. But no one stood at the upstairs window anymore. Because now he stood—just a couple of yards—in front of her, his handsome face stark with shock as the color drained from his usually dark skin. "Olivia…?"

He could see her.

This was what she'd wanted, she reminded herself, as panic choked her. She had wanted him to see her. She had *needed* him to see her to exact her revenge.

But when he lifted his arms and reached for her, the panic turned to fear. And she spun around, running along the shore.

"Olivia!"

The scrape of his shoes against the rocks warned her that he followed. And his ragged breath rising above the wind warned that he drew closer.

With dread she turned to the lake. Every time she went back in, she had to fight harder to reach the surface—to leave those icy depths. But while she'd wanted him to see her, she wasn't ready yet. She wasn't as strong as she needed to be to face *him*. She dove into the water, sinking fast as the lake, pulling at her gown and her hair, sucked her deep.

God, what had she done? Why had she run? It wasn't as if he could kill her twice. She was already dead....

The water shifted around her, as another body fought against the power of the lake. But this one was alive, for now. Damien's long legs and arms thrashed as he dove deep. Looking for her?

All these months of restless wandering, this was what she had wanted, for what she had waited. For him to see her. And for an opportunity for revenge. She would have no more perfect opportunity than now... than for him to experience the same fate she had.

Death.

Six months ago, on one night of their honeymoon, she had waited on the shore for him to return from checking in at the casino in Grayson. Wearing only her wedding-night negligee and moonlight, she had planned a special surprise for him. Anticipation had rushed through her as she'd heard the distinctive engine of his custom-made sports car pulling into the drive. But she hadn't anticipated the attack moments later. She'd had only a momentary flash of foreboding before the blow—not enough warning to react. To save herself and…

She had been knocked over the head and dumped into the lake. The icy water had shocked her into consciousness, and she had fought hard against the hands holding her beneath the water. *His hands.* She had clawed and kicked, trying to free herself. But then the water had filled her lungs, and she had lost her strength and consciousness again. She'd sunk deep to the bottom of the lake that legend claimed was bottomless. Because no one had ever reached such depths…and *lived.*

And this time, neither would he…

She cut through the water until she found him. He had changed direction now, kicking toward the surface, unwilling to dive as deep as he had sent her, as he had consigned her for eternity. And she reached out, manacling her fingers around his ankle.

This was the revenge she had wanted, she reminded herself, as doubts assailed her. This was what he deserved for what he had done to her. An eye for an eye…

A life for a life…

But he hadn't taken just one.

Lungs burning with oxygen deprivation, Damien fought his way toward the surface—toward air. But something caught his foot, wrapping around his ankle and pulling him down. Above him lightning flashed, illuminating the lake and those precious feet that separated him from the surface.

What the hell had he been thinking to leap into the Lake of Tears after an apparition? She couldn't be real. God, he was losing his mind. And now maybe his life…

He kicked with one foot, the other still caught. Something cold, but which paradoxically heated his blood, wound tight around his ankle, trapping him beneath the water. Panic pressed against his chest, adding to the constriction from lack of oxygen. He had to stay calm if he intended to stay alive.

But hell, what was the point of fighting, of *living,* when he had nothing for which—for *whom*—to live?

But he was a Gray—a Gray *Wolf,* actually, before his ancestors had dropped their surname. And through history Grays had always been fierce warriors. Damien could not stop fighting because he didn't know how; it was too much a part of his nature, the very essence of who and what he was.

Summoning the last of his energy, as unconsciousness threatened, his vision growing black, he turned in the water, diving down to see on what he was caught.

And he saw *her.* Pale—almost translucent— fingers wrapped around his ankle, trapping him under the water.

Why?

Her face lifted toward his, and their gazes met. Those pale blue eyes, which had once shone with love whenever she'd looked at him, were now hard and cold with hatred.

"Why?" he mouthed the word at her. And as he did, the last of his air left his lungs and his world went black, swallowing her ghostly image from his sight as the Lake of Tears swallowed his body.

The ancient ghost of an Indian shaman stood on the rocky slope, where he had died centuries ago, before a sorceress's tears had filled the deep ravine

*and formed the lake. And he watched and waited,
hoping that this time the Gray Wolf warrior would
not rise from the depths of the abyss and* live....

Chapter 2

Head pounding like the beat of an ancient war drum, Damien crept back to consciousness. His skin stung as the icy chill receded, chased away by the warmth of a blazing fire and a scratchy wool blanket. He knocked the blanket aside as he lifted his hand and pushed his shaking fingers through his still-damp hair.

"It was *real*," he murmured, his throat raspy with shock and cold.

"It was stupid," a deep voice grumbled as a man kicked shut the door of the small cabin and dropped chunks of wood onto the floor near the mammoth stone fireplace. "What the hell, man? What were you thinking?"

"Nathan…" Damien recognized the rough-hewn pine boards of the ceiling and the log walls of his cousin's cabin. The structure in the woods was even older than the house sitting on the rocky edge of the Lake of Tears. "You pulled me out?"

"Again," Nathan said.

He had been there last time—six months ago. He had dragged Damien, kicking and swinging, from the water and convinced him it was pointless to search for Olivia. He hadn't even known for certain that she'd drowned.

But Damien had found her robe and her shoes on the rocky shore. And he had guessed where she'd been.

And tonight, he knew for certain. She hadn't run off as Nathan had tried to convince him she had.

She was dead.

"You were there," Damien said as he pushed himself up, bracing his elbow on the arm of the couch on which he lay. "Again…"

"Lucky for you," Nathan said.

For a man who made his living gambling, Damien was actually remarkably unfortunate—in love. "Yeah, lucky for me…"

His cousin turned to him, his dark gaze penetrating. "Were you trying…to kill yourself?"

"God, no." But Olivia had tried to kill him. *Why?* Had she only grown to hate him that much after her death, or had she hated him before? Had her love been a lie?

"Then what the hell were you doing out there, in the lake," Nathan demanded to know with anger and concern, "in the middle of a *storm?*"

Head still pounding, Damien winced at the volume of his cousin's voice, and the memory of what had compelled him to risk the storm and the icy water of the Lake of Tears.

Her…

Not willing yet to share what—*who*—he had seen, he asked instead, "What were *you* doing out in the storm?"

"My *job*. I'm the caretaker here," Nathan reminded him. "*Your* caretaker."

Damien suspected his cousin didn't refer to the fact that Nathan worked for him but that he was worried about him, about how he'd been living, actually *barely* living, since Olivia had disappeared nearly six months ago.

"If you weren't trying to kill yourself," Nathan persisted, "what the hell were you doing? You know the lake is bottomless. Some of our ancestors believed it to be the portal to the other world."

"Hell," Damien uttered the word as more than a curse, as a destiny. He should have known better than to think he could ever find happiness. "Hell is where this place always sends me. I never should have brought her here—not after—"

"She wanted to come. You told me that," Nathan remembered. The man never forgot anything, nothing from his lifetime or from the lifetimes of the ancestors who had lived before him and Damien. "You said she wanted to spend your honeymoon here in the house on the lake."

And like a damn fool Damien had wanted to give her *everything* she wanted. "I should have told her no."

"But it was where you met…."

The first time he'd seen her had been on the rocky shore of the Lake of Tears. For years he had hated coming to the Victorian house on the lake, and he had only visited when absolutely necessary to meet with Nathan. If not for his cousin, he would have sold the estate long ago. But Nathan had convinced him it was Damien's legacy and that he was honor bound by their people to care for the lake and the property.

Damien had been cutting around the lake, heading

to the woods and Nathan's cabin, when he'd come upon her standing on the rocky shore. Even then he hadn't believed that she was real; she was far too beautiful to be simply human.

The summer wind played with her hair, whipping platinum-blond locks across her face and around her shoulders. She wore a linen vest, sleeveless and low cut that revealed the shadow between her breasts, and pants in the same pale blue of her eyes. The wind molded the linen to her curves, revealing more than it covered.

"You are the most beautiful trespasser I've ever had," Damien remarked with an appreciative whistle, drawing her from her contemplation of the lake.

Startled, she jumped and then turned toward him. And her eyes widened with surprise and something close to recognition, as if she knew him even though they had never met before.

The same sense of recognition jarred him. She looked like a *legend,* the spitting image of the woman whose story had been passed from generation to generation in his family. She looked like the woman whose tears over her murdered lover had created the lake. And whose supernatural ability to resurrect the dead had brought the Indian warrior—whose mission had been to kill her—back to life. A life they had shared on the rocky shore of the Lake of Tears.

"I'm not trespassing," she insisted, her chin lifting with pride and indignation.

Because the land had been hers first?

He shook his head, shaking off the fanciful thought he blamed on his cousin's fascination with the past. If not for his having to visit Nathan, Damien would not have even thought of the legend. But he wouldn't have met this woman, either. And, as a shiver of foreboding lifted the hair on the nape of his neck, he considered that *not* meeting her might have been a good thing. With a flash of prophecy to which he would never admit, he sensed that his life was about to change…because of *her.*

"Then what the hell are you doing on my property?" he asked, growling the question as he did when he wanted to intimidate someone.

She didn't lower her chin. She only narrowed her eyes and met his hard stare, unintimidated. "I'm checking out the wedding package."

"Wedding package?" He repeated her ridiculous excuse, almost disappointed that she hadn't come up with something more plausible.

"Yes, wedding package," she insisted. "The ad described it as a wedding ceremony on the shore of the beautiful Lake of Tears, performed by a real Indian shaman. And the reception in the dining room of the house." She gestured toward the Victorian on the hill. "And a honeymoon in the bridal suite in the second story of the turret."

Damien's breath caught with a stabbing pain in his chest. Damn, now he knew why Nathan had insisted on a meeting. He'd hatched another of his hair-brained schemes. But this one…

How could his cousin have ever considered opening up the lake and the house to the public a good idea? How could he think Damien would go along with such a thing…? How would reducing their heritage to a reception hall honor their *legacy,* their *people?*

"Are you all right?" she asked.

Her question surprised him. In all of his thirty-six years, he had never met anyone, besides his cousin, who had been able to read his moods. Not even his wife, despite all the years they'd known each other, had ever really understood him.

"I'm fine," he said, "just trying to figure out if you're lying…."

Or if all the years of Nathan drinking the potions he concocted from the plants and flowers growing wild on the land had finally reduced him to madness…

Again the indignation flashed in her light-blue eyes. "I am *not* lying."

"But why would you be checking out wedding packages—" he was going to kill Nathan; all the shaman's herbs and roots and potions were not going to save him from Damien's rage "—when you're not wearing a ring?" He stepped close, caught her hand in his and held up her bare fingers.

God, her skin was silky…

"I gave the engagement ring back to my fiancé—my ex-fiancé." She expelled a ragged breath and lifted her gaze to Damien's. "But now…I don't know…."

At the thought of her wearing another man's ring, Damien tensed and tightened his grasp on her hand. "But you had some doubts…."

She nodded. "I'm not sure they were really *my* doubts, though, or…"

"If you had *any* doubts, you did the right thing," he assured her, "by returning his ring."

He'd had doubts, and now he wished like hell he hadn't ignored them. But Melanie had fallen for him when he'd been a poor Indian kid on a college scholarship with nothing else to his name. And then she'd stuck by him through all those long, empty days and nights while he had been working to establish his career. Guilt gripped him, as it always did, when he acknowledged that he hadn't been there for her when she had needed him most.

The blond-haired woman tugged at her hand, trying to free it from his. But instead of releasing her, he entwined their fingers. "So since you don't intend to use the wedding package, you're here under false pretenses," he pointed out. "You are trespassing."

"What are you going to do?" she asked, her voice soft with challenge. "Call the sheriff?"

Even if the nearby village of Grayson had an active sheriff, calling him wouldn't have been Damien's first inclination. His first inclination of how to handle his beautiful trespasser had his blood pumping faster through his veins...in anticipation.

He shook his head. "Nope. *My land. My law.*"

"Hmmm..." she mused, pursing her full lips, "I don't remember that law being on the bar exam."

"Did you pass?" he asked, his tone doubtful even though he believed she would not have brought up the exam if she hadn't passed.

Her chin rose a little higher with pride and a touch of arrogance that intrigued him as much as her beauty did. "First time."

"So you're smart *and* beautiful," he concluded.

"Brilliant," she bragged with a self-deprecating grin that mocked her own ego.

"And modest," he teased.

She shrugged those sexy bare shoulders. "I don't have time for modesty."

"In that case maybe you decided to trespass in order to skinny-dip in the lake. So don't let me stop you." He released her hand but reached for the buttons on her vest.

She grabbed his wrists, her breath coming fast through her parted lips. "Don't! Don't—"

"Oh, would you rather I go first?" He stepped back and pulled his shirt over his head, dropping the black cashmere onto the rocky shore.

Her eyes wide, she stared at his chest. "I—I—uh…" she stammered then slid the tip of her pink tongue across her bottom lip.

"I hope you're more eloquent than that in court." He reached for his belt.

"Don't!" she yelled again. "Don't take off anything else. I'm not here to skinny-dip."

"Or for a wedding," he reminded her. Because the Lake of Tears would become a wedding spot only over his dead body.

"I'm here because I'm curious about the lake," she admitted. But she didn't so much as glance at the water, her attention still focused on his bare chest.

"So let me satisfy your *curiosity*." He stepped closer and she jerked her gaze to his face.

"A-about the lake," she stammered.

"Of course. About the lake," he agreed, unable to keep a grin from his mouth. "What do you want to know?"

"You don't want to put your shirt back on?" she asked, her voice soft and wistful.

He shook his head. "It's hot."

"No, it's not," she protested, shivering in the light summer breeze.

"You're from the Lower Peninsula," he surmised. "Downstate."

"Detroit."

He would have guessed. She had an urban air about her—one of glamour and sophistication. All the things he had fought so hard to become she had probably been born.

"I'm thinking about moving up here, though," she shared, her gaze watchful as if she cared what he thought.

"To get away from the ex?" he asked, wondering about her broken engagement.

"To be *here*." She gestured toward the lake. "Somehow I think I belong here. I know that probably sounds crazy…."

What was crazy was the way she made him feel— as if she belonged with *him*.

"I don't even know your name," he realized.

"Olivia Kingston." She held out her hand.

Instead of shaking, he lifted it to his mouth and brushed his lips across her knuckles. She shivered again.

"And you are?" she asked.

"Your destiny," he answered her.

She smiled. "Apparently I'm not the only one who doesn't have time for modesty."

He didn't have time for a lot of things—actually for anything or anyone outside the casinos he ran throughout Michigan. But yet something about her compelled him to make time…for her. "I'm Damien Gray."

She laughed. "Of course you are. No wonder you don't have time for modesty." Her laughter evaporated like water on the hot rocks. "And you don't have time for my questions, either. I'm sorry to have bothered you…."

She stepped forward as if she intended to move around him and head up the hill to the house and the street beyond it. But he caught her, wrapping his hand around her bare arm. Goose bumps rose on her skin beneath his palm.

"You have bothered me," he admitted, resenting how she had opened up his world to possibilities again. "But you're going to bother me more if you leave now." Because then he would never know what might have become of those possibilities.

"I don't think it's a good idea for me stay," she said, and for the first time fear flickered in her eyes.

"Why?" he asked, lowering his voice. "Afraid I might talk you into skinny-dipping?"

Her gaze slid over his bare chest again, and with a heavy sigh, she confessed, "I'm afraid you might talk me into all kinds of things."

Later, after he'd told her Gray Wolf and Anya's legend of the Lake of Tears, he had talked her into skinny-dipping.

Playing naked in the water with her that day had been a far cry from tonight—when she had tried to kill him.

"Hey!" Nathan shouted, snapping his fingers in Damien's face. "Are you all right?"

Pushing back his memories, Damien focused on his cousin and nodded. "Yeah, yeah, I'm fine…"

Nathan studied him, clearly unconvinced. "I thought I lost you again."

"No, I'm here," Damien assured him. "Thanks to you." His breath shuddered out in a ragged sigh. "Thanks for pulling me out."

During the summers they had spent at the Lake of

Tears, staying with their grandfather in the old Victorian, which had been pretty dilapidated then, he and Nathan had grown as close as brothers. Nathan had always been there for him, even after Damien, as the oldest grandson, had inherited the house and the lake when their grandfather passed. Nathan had loved and understood the land and the legend more than Damien ever would. But maybe that was why he didn't care that he didn't own the estate; his job as caretaker was more important.

"So what the hell happened tonight?" Nathan asked, dropping onto the wooden crate that served as his coffee table. "Tell me what's going on with you."

Damien grimaced at the persistent pounding inside his head. Stalling, he pushed a hand through his hair again. "I wish to hell I knew."

"Well, what brought you out of the house during the storm?" Nathan asked, speaking softly and slowly as if he feared his cousin had lost his mind.

Damien drew in a deep breath. God, it was bad enough *he* thought he was crazy, but to share what had happened with anyone else…

But then no one else would understand like Nathan, who claimed to be able to see a ghost himself, of a long-dead shaman who served as his spirit guide, advising him in using the plants and flowers that grew wild on the land. Only on this land.

"I've been seeing her," he admitted.

"Who?" Nathan asked, his brows arched. "You're dating someone?"

The thought of seeing someone besides Olivia struck Damien like a spear through the heart. He couldn't betray her. But tonight, tugging him under, she had done more than betray him.

"I've been seeing *Olivia*...."

Nathan stilled, his body tense. "She's come back to the Lake of Tears?"

Damien shook his head. "No, she never left."

"Then I don't understand.... If you're so convinced she's dead, how could you..." He trailed off, his mouth dropping open in surprise. "You think you've seen her ghost?"

Damien released a ragged breath. "I wasn't sure. Over the past six months, I've been catching glimpses of something down by the lake." A wisp of smoke when the sky was clear. An orb of sunlight when the sky was dark. But tonight she had taken shape, the same gorgeous shape she'd had when she lived. "Of someone..."

"So now you're sure?" Nathan asked, his voice guarded as if he was still unconvinced.

But Damien had no doubts. "Yes."

His cousin's brow furrowed. "I don't understand. Why would she come back?"

The pounding in Damien's head repeated in his heart, which ached as he recalled the look in her eyes as she had trapped him underwater—that look of utter hatred. "To kill me."

Shock widened Nathan's eyes. "What?"

"She tried to kill me tonight."

"In the lake?" His cousin shook his head. "Damien, that doesn't make sense. A spirit can't touch you, can't hurt you…"

"I felt her." He swallowed hard. His skin tingled yet from where she had clutched his ankle. "I felt her fingers around my ankle. I felt *her*. She wasn't real—she wasn't human—but she *was*. You know what I mean?"

His expression guarded, Nathan replied, "I know you've been under a lot of stress since she disappeared."

"You think I'm going crazy?"

His cousin's gaze dropped away from his. "I know you were crazy in love with Olivia, even more than you ever loved Melanie."

Catching the censure in Nathan's tone, Damien struggled to explain. "Melanie was my friend. She was faithful. She stuck by me."

"You talk about her like she was a dog," Nathan remarked, his voice sharp with resentment. With all the time Melanie had spent alone at the lake while Damien worked, she had grown close to his cousin.

"She'd been a part of my life for so long," Damien said. "She was important to me."

"Not as important as Olivia."

"Olivia was my fate." Maybe he shouldn't have fought tonight. Maybe he should have succumbed to his fate. "She was my *destiny*." And he should have told her that while she was alive; he should have opened up his heart to her and truly gave her the *everything* he had promised her on their wedding night. "Surely you can understand that, Nathan."

"I understand that you need to get away from here," the shaman counseled him, as he counseled so many of the townspeople.

But the difference was that the townspeople *believed*. Even after tonight, after seeing a ghost himself, Damien struggled to accept otherworldly powers or abilities.

Nathan stood up and returned to the fire, staring into the flames. "You need to get back to work."

"I go to work."

"What? A few times a week? Your job used to

consume your life. You need to let it consume you again," Nathan advised, "before *she* does."

Damien didn't bother telling his cousin that it was already too late. If Nathan were really a shaman, he knew.

Olivia consumed him. Thoughts of her haunted him day and night. And now her ghost haunted him.

"Can't you help me?" Damien asked. "This— *spirits*—that's your thing, your area of expertise."

Nathan chuckled. "So you believe me *now?* You must be desperate."

"I am," Damien admitted, knowing he deserved his cousin's derision. He had treated him to more than enough of his disbelief over the years, when he'd been unable to accept that Nathan had any special abilities. But Nathan had never been offended, not even when Damien had raged at him over his plans to perform weddings on the shore of the Lake of Tears—where Nathan had married him and Melanie and where she had died years later on the rocky hill above the lake. Damien had been furious, and Nathan had apologized, respecting Damien's wishes to keep the tragedy private.

Nathan had always understood and, Damien suspected, pitied him for not being able to believe in the magic of the land the young shaman considered sacred and of the special abilities of their people—of *him.*

"Can't you help me?" he implored his cousin.

Nathan shook his head. "I wish there was some drink I could make you. Some talisman I could give you. But even I can't find a cure for a broken heart, man."

"You think that's what's going on with me? You don't think I really saw her tonight?"

His cousin shrugged. "I don't know, Damien. You've never seen *anything* before, and this land is alive with the energy of the spirits of all our ancestors who passed. Why would you see *only* her?"

"Because I love her." Even now, even after what she'd done tonight.

Nathan nodded. "And because of that, you don't want to let her go."

"I can't."

"And that's probably why, if you really saw her ghost, that she's still here," the shaman explained. "Because you won't let her go. You're holding her back from crossing over."

Could that be why she hated him now?

"How do I let her go?"

Nathan shrugged again. "You need time, but more importantly, you need distance. You hardly came around here after Melanie died. And that helped you get over her."

Olivia, and really falling in love for the first time, had helped him get over the senseless death of his first wife. "I won't get over Olivia."

"Not if you don't try," Nathan agreed. "You need to get the hell out of here."

Damien shook his head. He couldn't leave her…even if she hated him.

Chapter 3

The Wise One stood on the rocky bluff where he had died centuries ago, before the lake had formed from the sorceress's tears. Like then, when a dagger had pierced his heart, he felt his power slipping away. Once again a Gray Wolf warrior threatened to disrupt his plan—over a woman.

She was dead. Did she not know it? She wandered the lake and the land as if unaware she had been killed. And she remained unaware of his presence, as if she were more real than him, as if she were more human than ghost.

Or was she, like the long-dead woman she eerily resembled, a sorceress? Fear flickered through him like a flame, but he snuffed out the fire with reason. If she were a sorceress, she would have been able to save herself or to bring herself back as a flesh-and-blood woman rather than a ghost.

No, this woman had no more power than any other mere mortal. The only way the Wise One suspected she was like him was that she had some unfinished business trapping her in this world. And perhaps he could use that, and use her as he had used others, to help him—at long last—complete his mission.

Maybe she could have passed through the walls. But since she wasn't certain of the limitations of being a ghost, Olivia opened the front door. She stared down at her hand on the knob, surprised she had enough strength to turn it. Until last night, when Damien had finally seen her by the lake, she hadn't been strong enough or substantial enough to even create a ripple across the surface of the water. Until she had grabbed his ankle, touching him, she hadn't had enough strength to hold on to or move anything. But now she was strong—strong enough to do what she needed to do.

She stepped inside the house, wincing as the

mahogany door closed behind her and the click of the lock echoed in the two-story foyer. As moved by the beauty of the house as she had been the first time she'd seen it, Olivia stared in awe at the chandelier hanging above her. Light caught in the crystal prisms and bounced off the gleaming marble floor in myriad colors.

How could a man responsible for such beauty be capable of so much ugliness? She had seen the "before" pictures and had lived in the "after." She knew the money and time Damien had spent restoring the house after it had fallen into a state of disrepair when his grandfather had owned it.

Another man might have torn down the home that had succumbed to the harsh elements of the Upper Peninsula. Tearing down and building new would have been cheaper and easier. But Damien never did what was easy.

And killing him wouldn't be easy, either. She should have known he would fight. Yet, had he broken free of her hold, or had she let him go last night?

Guilt tempered her anger as she recalled the look in his eyes—the utter shock and…

Devastation?

Had she hurt him? She would not have considered it possible to hurt a man as tough and independent as Damien Gray. But then what did she really know about the man she had married in such a hurry?

That he was incredibly charismatic. She had never been as immediately drawn to another human being. Even now embarrassment filled her that she had made love with him the first day they'd met. She had dated her ex-fiancé for months before finally, after much deliberation, deciding to take their relationship to the next level.

With Damien, she had never deliberated. She had never thought at all. Until now. When it was too late. Anger rushed through her, energizing her. But this time she was mad at herself as she silently admitted to letting him go last night. She had released him—unable to kill him. Her anger turned to disgust. For six months she had plotted her revenge—and not just for herself.

She glided her palm over her stomach. Her whole body was empty now—with no substance, like her. She had been so weak to let him go just because of how he'd looked at her. And how he'd made her feel…

When Olivia had worked in the prosecutor's office in Detroit, she had never understood those women who refused to testify against the husbands or boy-friends who had abused them and then returned to these men when they were released from jail. Was she one of those women—so obsessed with Damien that she would go back to him if she were able?

If she were alive…

No. She was smarter than that—stronger than that. She had only changed her mind about killing him because she needed more proof of his guilt first.

She had only heard his car that night, coming up the drive. She hadn't heard him creep up behind her moments later. But only Damien moved that silently, as silently as whoever had struck her over the head as she waited for her new husband beside the lake. She'd had only a brief flash of dread, goose bumps lifting her skin, which she'd attributed to the chill air, before she'd been struck. And when she was in the water, sinking to the icy depths, she'd *felt* him. His presence was unmistakable.

He had been there—close. Yet she hadn't actually seen him. Even if she could testify against him, her testimony would not be enough to convict him. Not without more evidence.

Hope filled her that she would find the evidence she needed and *not* Damien in the house. She didn't want to see him again until she knew for certain if she'd been wrong about him when they had met and she'd fallen so fast for him, or if she was wrong about him now thinking him a killer.

She passed through the foyer, with its rich, champagne-hued brocade wallpaper, and headed up the curved staircase, with the hand-carved mahogany banister, to the second story. Sunlight poured through the stained-glass window onto the landing, casting a rainbow of color across the polished mahogany steps. Nerves added to her restlessness as she left the staircase and headed down the wide center hall. Her steps slowed on the gleaming hardwood as she neared the master suite. She reached out to push open the door, her fingers curling into her palm, forming a fist.

But the room was empty. So Olivia had only to fight the emotions flooding her like the sunshine flooding the room through the curved turret windows. This room was papered, too, in a mint-green paisley pattern that complemented the dark hardwood floor and moldings.

She closed her mind to the memories threatening to overwhelm her and crossed the threshold. Ignoring the sleigh bed, she crossed to the antique dresser in the same deep mahogany and opened drawers. She found her clothes folded exactly as she had put them away. Damien hadn't packed them up or thrown them out. He had left all her belongings—as if he'd expected her to come back.

But if he had killed her, how could he have considered that possible? If he had killed her, he would have to know she could only return as a ghost. She tamped down her faint hope in his innocence, unwilling to draw any more conclusions based on emotion instead of evidence.

Then, despite the clear day, the windows rattled. Not from the force of the wind but from the power of the vehicle roaring up the driveway, with the same distinctive engine Olivia had heard that fateful night.

Damien had had the sports car custom designed. She knew no other vehicle, especially in the rural area of Grayson, that sounded the least bit similar. Only his vehicle sounded like the dangerous snarl of a wolf as it leaped to attack.

Like he had attacked her that night?

Did she need more evidence to convict him in her mind? She hadn't thought so, but then she remembered his face in the water—the shock, the pain of what he must have considered her betrayal....

If not for that look, she would have tried again for her revenge. Did she have enough strength to cut his brake line, so when he drove, as he always did, too fast around the hairpin turns to the lake, he would lose control? But Damien Gray rarely lost control.

The front door slammed and his feet pounded on the stairs, heading up to the bedroom. And her. She could have rushed out and pushed him down the stairs. But he was so fit, so muscular, that he would probably survive the fall.

Could she kill him—even if she found the evidence that proved, beyond a doubt, his guilt? Was it possible to kill a man as powerful as Damien Gray?

His footsteps grew louder and closer.

She gasped, realizing she had frozen again, like she had on the shore the night before. And like then, she panicked again. Without the lake to leap into, she could only scramble for a place to hide, ducking into the luxurious bathroom and then the walk-in closet off the master bath.

Before she could draw the door closed, he stepped into the bathroom, his shoes scraping against the marble-tile floor. She couldn't close the door without him noticing, so she moved back into a rack of clothes, hiding behind an assortment of dresses she'd brought to the house. She had packed more things than she'd needed for just their honeymoon, but she'd wanted to talk Damien into moving permanently to the house on the Lake of Tears. To her it had always felt more like home than the townhouse he owned in the condo development adjacent to the casino in Grayson.

Yet, despite promising to give her everything she wanted, Damien had refused to move to the Victorian, and had even seemed uneasy staying in the house the short time they had before she died. But now, after she was gone, he had remained. Alone.

Or he had been alone before her return from the dead? Through the dresses, she caught his reflection in the mirror on the open door of the closet. And a sensation, very much like a quickening of her blood, raced through her. While her body was gone, she still had the feelings—*all the feelings*—she'd had before her death.

Even for him...

He was so damn handsome. Dressed as he was in a suit and tie, he must have been at the casino. His hand jerked at the silver tie, pulling it free of the collar of the shirt in nearly the same shade of silver. The silk fabric shimmered, molding to his chest as he cast off his suit jacket, dropping it into a wicker basket for dry-cleaning.

Then his fingers undid the buttons of the shirt, and he tugged the silk free of his pants and cast off that garment, too, leaving his chest bare. Sunlight poured through an octagon window and painted gold the sculpted muscles of his smooth chest.

His hand went to his belt now, pulling it free of his black dress pants. He draped the belt across the corner of the marble vanity, then dropped his wallet and cell phone beside it before unzipping his pants. He pushed down his briefs along with his pants, his hands skimming down the sides of his lean hips.

Olivia closed her eyes on the image of his dimpled backside reflecting back from the mirror. But she couldn't keep them closed; she had to be aware of where he was, if he was about to discover her hiding in the closet.

But he hadn't moved toward the door. Instead, water sputtered and then ran as he turned on the faucet in the shower. Muscles rippled in his back and arms as he leaned out of the glass enclosure and lifted his hand to the thick, black hair bound at the base of his neck. He pulled free the leather thong holding it, and the hair skimmed his broad shoulders.

Despite her anger and resentment, desire pulsed through Olivia—warming and energizing her. Making her stronger and more substantial. How could she still want him? Had she lost her mind along with her life?

He stepped inside the shower, but the glass enclosure did not conceal his body; it only framed the masculine perfection that was Damien Gray. Water sluiced over his smooth, dark skin and rippling muscles. Olivia's gaze followed drops of water from his sharp cheekbones, over the line of his strong jaw, down the impressive muscles of his chest, over the ripple of his washboard abs to where it caught in the dark hair around his manhood. Even though his penis wasn't hard, it was still impressive—hanging heavy against his lean thighs.

Olivia closed her eyes again, trying to shut out the image…and the memories that pummeled her—of all those mornings and evenings she had joined him in that shower, soaping up every sexy inch of his body. She'd never been able to keep her gaze or her hands off him. He was so beautiful. She hadn't believed he'd really been hers. And in the end, he hadn't been—not if he'd been the one who had killed her.

But she forgot that as she watched him run soap over his skin. She flashed back to those times she had stepped inside the shower with him. To when she'd pressed a kiss between his shoulder blades, running her lips down the length of his sexy spine.

He would whirl around, catching her close— pulling her tight into his arms so that his chest crushed her breasts. And he cupped her face in his hands, tipping it up so that his mouth could devour hers. His lips pressed hers apart, so his tongue could slide inside, tasting and teasing her. Then, with his wet skin sliding against hers, he lifted her, making love to her against the glass, which steamed up not from the moisture of the shower but from the heat of their unquenchable passion.

Even now, knowing what he had undoubtedly done to her, she wanted him. How could she be so weak?

As the shower shut off, she tensed. But yet she couldn't look away from the reflection in the mirror as he stepped out, droplets of water trailing down his body. He reached for a towel, sliding the soft, white terry cloth over every inch of his dark skin.

Energy charged throughout Olivia with her desire. She glanced down at herself, surprised to find her image so substantial—nearly as real as his.

Dropping the towel into a hamper, he sauntered naked into the walk-in closet. As he reached for jeans and a shirt, he stood so close that Olivia noticed when goose bumps rose on the smooth skin of his broad back, along the spine she had once kissed so tenderly. And he whirled around, turning toward her.

She stilled, cowering behind the long dresses. And she hated herself for cowering, and she hated him for making her cower. But it was like last night—on the shore—she wasn't ready to *see* him. She needed proof first.

"Olivia? Olivia, are you here?" Damien asked in his deep, soft voice.

Even though she had no real breath to hold, Olivia

held it—willing herself invisible to him now, when for six months she had been desperate for him to see her image.

Damien pushed a slightly shaking hand through his wet hair. "God, you're losing it, man," he murmured to himself. "Nathan's right—you need to get out of here."

No! Olivia held in the shout—barely—but it echoed in her mind. He couldn't leave yet, not until she found the evidence that proved his guilt or innocence. If he left, she would never have justice. She would be forever trapped in the Lake of Tears.

Like she was trapped right now in the closet with him. But he dressed quickly, pulling on jeans and dragging a dark T-shirt over his head. The cotton clung to his damp skin, molded to his chest. Naked or clothed, the man affected her like no other man ever had.

Had her attraction to him blinded her to his faults, to the dangerous side of him that others had warned her about?

With one last glance around the closet, he walked out the door. Moments later she heard his footfalls on the mahogany treads of the staircase. And again a door opened and closed.

If she'd had breath, Olivia would have released it. Her tension eased with relief that he was gone. She stepped out from behind her dresses and moved back into the bathroom. Peering out the octagonal window, she glimpsed him below, walking down the rocky hill toward the lake. Sunlight gleamed in his dark hair, the wind ruffling and drying the long mane that hung loose around his shoulders.

She pulled her gaze from him, resolving that he would not distract her again. But then she noticed his clothes spilling out of the basket. And she lifted his shirt.

Had he been at the casino—where the female employees fawned over him and the female customers drooled? When Olivia had started working there, she had been warned that he was a womanizer, that after his wife's tragic death, he had no relationships—only one-night stands. She had disregarded the warnings, writing them off as the jealousy of her fellow workers.

But now she wondered. Had he gotten rid of Olivia because he had changed his mind about being tied to one woman?

Freedom was his likeliest motive for murder. Olivia had owed more money than she had, and he had taken out no life insurance on her. So he couldn't have murdered her for financial gain. But maybe he had done it to avoid financial loss. They had married in such haste that he had never asked her to sign a prenup, as a man with his substantial wealth should have done. But maybe he hadn't considered one necessary, as he preferred murder to divorce.

And freedom to marriage?

She brought his shirt to her face and inhaled deeply. But no feminine perfume emanated from the silk. Only his musky aftershave clung to the material. But that didn't really prove anything—that didn't mean he wasn't seeing other women.

But when? Over the past six months, she'd noted that he rarely left the house. So she had to make the most of this opportunity before he interrupted her again. She dropped the shirt and turned away from the window.

And she resumed her search for evidence of his guilt. Upstairs she rummaged through closets and dresser drawers. She even checked the attic, glancing inside boxes—hoping to find some evidence of not just her murder but Melanie's, too.

If he had killed his second wife, he had probably killed his first wife. As with the warnings about his womanizing, Olivia had been warned that he was a killer, as well. But she had been too in love, or too infatuated, to listen to any of the warnings.

And she had believed Damien when he'd claimed that Melanie had killed herself. Was that what he had told people about Olivia—that she had taken her own life? Anger surged through her, strengthening her energy and her resolve as she continued her search.

Downstairs she checked cupboards and desk drawers. She did not exactly know what she was looking for, but yet she realized she had found it when she pulled a search warrant from atop the pile of papers on the desk in Damien's mahogany-paneled den. The round room was in the turret beneath the master bedroom—its curved windows framing the lake and the man who stood on the shore of it, gazing out over the water.

Olivia pulled her gaze from him to focus on the warrant, which encompassed the house, grounds and lake. So the police had searched for her body, but she'd sunk too deep. Even if they had dredged, they wouldn't have found her.

Had they found anything else for which they'd searched—any evidence of a homicide? *Her* homicide? Or Melanie's?

Apparently she was not the only one who suspected Damien of killing her. But if the police had found the evidence they needed, he would not be a free man right now.

Of course he was too smart to leave any evidence. He was too smart to get caught.

But maybe he had left a witness—one more reliable and able to testify than she was. Ignoring a pang of loss and regret, she left the house and, avoiding the lake beneath which her body lay and where Damien stood vigil, she slipped deep into the woods.

And she hoped he wasn't the only one who could see her....

Chapter 4

Moving with inherit stealth, Damien crept through the woods—his attention on the trail ahead and the woman who followed it, on her way from the house. He had thought he'd sensed her presence inside—while he'd been taking his shower.

He had felt her gaze on him, watching him as he had often caught her watching him—her blue eyes bright with desire. And he would open the door of the shower and pull her inside with him, her squealing as the water saturated the clothes she wore. But he'd help her, quickly, out of the wet garments. Baring all her pale skin to the pulse of the water and the caress of his hands…and his mouth…

He was always thorough, missing no delectable inch of her, licking the water from her breasts, running his tongue in circles around her pouting nipples before closing his lips around one.

She would moan and tangle her fingers in his hair while he moved his fingers lower, between her thighs, through her curls to her very core.

"Damien!" He could hear her yet, screaming his name as she came.

But he never allowed her time to catch her breath before he lifted her, thrusting inside her wet heat. Her legs locked tight around his waist, she would arch her hips—in perfect rhythm with his thrusts—until they both screamed in passionate release.

He expelled a ragged breath. God, it had been too long since he'd had that release. With Olivia gone he'd had no desire to make love because he had no one to love with her gone.

But was she really gone?

He focused on the woman ahead of him on the trail. Her hair the color of moonlight, she had to be Olivia, but yet she looked more substantial, more real, than the woman from the lake the night before.

Was his bride alive and only trying to drive him

out of his mind? His gut tightened with dread as he realized he should have known better than to take the risk of trusting her. He was a gambler—not a fool.

He quickened his pace, closing the distance between them. But she did not hear his approach, nor sense his presence. So he reached out and grabbed her arm, whirling her toward him. His breath shuddered out, and he murmured, "You're not Olivia…."

But with her platinum hair and blue eyes, the older woman looked eerily similar to Damien's bride. Even the look in her eyes—of resentment and hatred—matched the look Damien had seen in Olivia's when she had tried to kill him the night before.

Yet this woman was much more petite than his bride. Olivia had sexy, long legs, which had brought her head to the level of his chin—so he'd only had to dip down a little to take her mouth with his.

"No," she said, growling the word at him. "Because of you, Olivia is gone. You killed her!" She lashed out at him with her fists, pummeling his chest.

Damien caught her thin wrists, pulling her hands away from him. "Who are you?"—that she looked so much like Olivia.

Beyond the hair, which could have been dyed, she had the same eyes, the same delicately featured face.

But lines rimmed her mouth and creased her eyes, under which circles darkened the pale skin.

"Who are you?" he asked again.

"Ana Olsson."

He furrowed his brow; her name meant nothing to him. "Who are you…to my wife?"

"I am—" Her breath caught as pain flashed through her eyes. "I *was*—her mother."

Damien studied the strange woman, who wore a loose-fitting green dress, as if she'd wanted to blend into the woods, as if she'd wanted to go undiscovered. He tried to gauge if she spoke the truth.

He hadn't yet met Olivia's parents—there hadn't been time, not with how quickly they'd married. But he had seen a photograph Olivia had kept on her desk at the casino—of a distinguished gray-haired man and a petite dark-haired woman flanking Olivia at her law-school graduation.

"She never told me about you," he said. But the woman was obviously her birth mother.

Pain pinched the older woman's face into a grimace. "I told her about *you*. I warned her that you would kill her. But she didn't listen to me, she married you anyways."

Tears pooled in her light-blue eyes, spilling down her face. "And now she's gone. She's dead." She tugged at her wrists, trying to free herself from his grip—no doubt to beat him some more.

"I did *not* kill Olivia," he insisted, and he tamped down his anger so he could control the urge to shake the woman. "I loved her."

And he had thought she'd loved him. But now he suspected he had been wrong—very wrong about Olivia.

"I saw what you did to her," Ana claimed, her voice cracking with emotion. "I saw you kill her. You *killed* her, you monster!"

No wonder Olivia had never mentioned anything about her biological mother; the woman was obviously crazy.

He shook her, just enough to snap her out of her hysteria. "What the hell are you talking about?"

"My *vision*," she said, trembling. "I had a vision of you killing my daughter, my baby."

"A vision?"

She nodded. "I have visions—of things that are yet to happen."

"You're a psychic?" he asked, hiding his skepticism. Even if he accepted the supernatural, he could not believe this woman, because what she claimed was a *lie*. He was *not* the one who had killed his bride. "You saw Olivia's death?"

"Murder," she said, spitting the word out with venom. "I saw you kill her. You knocked her over the head and then you drowned her in the…" Her voice caught as she choked on emotion. "You drowned her in the Lake of Tears."

"I didn't—"

"The Lake of Tears," she murmured again, as if the legendary waters meant something to her, too.

Like her daughter, she resembled the woman from the legend—with pale skin and hair and those eerily light blue eyes. But was her appearance natural or enhanced? Had she had her hair dyed and wore special contacts in order to resemble Anya?

He should have suspected before that Olivia might not have been what she appeared. He should have questioned *how* she had appeared to him, that first day they'd met when she had trespassed onto his property in order to see the lake. Had it all been a scam?

In the years since Melanie's death, quite a few women had tried to seduce him. They had been after his money more than his heart, though. Had he been naïve to believe that Olivia had been different, that she had actually loved him?

"I didn't do anything to Olivia," he insisted. Except fall for her.

Her mother continued speaking, as if she hadn't

heard him or as though she didn't care what he said. "I came to warn her, but she didn't listen to me. My ex-husband—her father—brainwashed her against me, after he took her from me."

"Like you apparently tried to brainwash her against me," he mused. "But when…?"

He and Olivia had only dated a few months before they'd married. She had been dead now longer than they had been together.

"I warned her a while ago," she said. "I haven't seen her since. And now—"

"Why are you here?" he asked. He hadn't held a memorial service for Olivia except for the bronze plate he'd had affixed to the boulder and the flowers he tossed across the lake—when he regretted not having given her more flowers when she was alive.

Her father, however, had held a service in Detroit, but Damien hadn't attended. Maybe Nathan was right—and his unwillingness to let her go was what trapped her in this world, between life and death….

"I need to be *here*," Ana Olsson insisted, gesturing back toward the lake that was visible between the trees. Tears glistened in her eyes. "I need to be near her."

He nodded. "I understand."

That was why he hadn't been able to leave the house he hated.

"I need to make sure she gets the justice she deserves," she said, the heat of anger drying the tears in her eyes. "I need to make sure you pay for what you did to her."

The sheriff had been hassling him, but Damien doubted it had anything to do with any pressure Olivia's mother might have exerted on the guy. No, Sheriff Haynes had his own motives for trying to put Damien away for something he had not done.

Damien clenched his jaw until a muscle jerked in his cheek. Then, expelling a deep breath, he said again, "I didn't do anything to her, but still I'm paying."

"You're not paying enough," she said.

Was that really why Ana Olsson was here? To shake him down for money?

But then, her voice quavering with anger and grief, she continued, "You're alive and Olivia is not…."

He narrowed his eyes to study her face as he asked, "You can't see her?"

The older woman's brow furrowed, and she gazed up at him as if he were the crazy one. "She's dead."

"But you can't…*see* her?"

"What do you mean?" She tilted her head. "Are you talking about her ghost?"

"Yeah." He nodded. "Can't a psychic see ghosts?"

"No." She sighed. "My visions are my only gift. But my maternal grandmother could see ghosts."

"So these…*gifts*…run in the family?" Nathan claimed the same thing, that he had inherited his shaman abilities from a shaman ancestor who had died centuries ago. "Did Olivia have a…gift?" Was that how she had come back from the dead to haunt him?

Her mother shook her head. "No, the ability skips a generation. Only one female of every other generation is born with a gift."

Damien bit his lip, holding back his reaction to her claim. Obviously the woman was quite familiar with the legend of the Lake of Tears and of the woman whose tears had created the body of water from a steep ravine. Anya, who had traveled with invaders from a faraway land, had had such an ability. Hers had been resurrecting the dead; that gift was why the warriors had taken her from her family and forced her to go into battles with them. If Anya had had a granddaughter, that child would have inherited a gift. But only sons had been born for generations of Gray Wolfs.

Olivia and her mother could not be descendents of Anya's—any more than he was. Damien had descended from the child that Gray Wolf had had before Anya had come to this land. But Anya had claimed the motherless child as her own, loving him with the same generosity and loyalty with which she had loved her Gray Wolf warrior.

Had Ana Olsson heard the legend of the Lake of Tears and claimed Anya's history as her own? Damien suspected as much. And he knew the strange woman couldn't help him. Apparently estranged from her daughter, she knew less of Olivia than he did.

He released her and stepped back, tense and ready in case she launched herself at him again. But the fight had gone out of her, and she just stood there as he turned and walked away.

Mist had already gathered on the surface of the lake. But he concentrated on the rocky shore as he headed for the house. He didn't want to see Olivia anymore.

Hell, Nathan was right—he needed to leave. He needed to finally let her go. Maybe without his holding her to this world, she would find peace. Something he doubted he would ever know again.

Olivia found the trail down which Damien had taken her once, after their marriage, to his cousin's home. She had asked Damien then why the caretaker didn't live in the carriage house or one of the many extra bedrooms in the main house. And he had explained that Nathan preferred the woods, that he felt closer to the land and his spirit guide.

She found the self-proclaimed shaman, not inside his rustic cabin, but outside at a clearing in the forest of pines. He sat, cross-legged on the ground, at the edge of a circle of fire.

Nathan shared Damien's dark hair and eyes, but the similarity between the cousins ended with their coloring. Nathan was smaller in stature and presence. And while Damien was debonair and worldly, the shaman was otherworldly. He wore brown suede pants and moccasins, his chest bare but for the streaks of something red—which matched the streaks across his face and forehead. Blood?

Olivia shuddered. God, she hoped he hadn't killed something. While the townspeople revered and trusted the shaman, Olivia didn't know if she should. Something about the man unsettled her. If only she had someone else she could turn to for help….

But maybe she could trust the shaman—probably more than she could trust her own instincts, which had failed her before.

"Nathan?" she softly whispered his name, worried about disturbing his intense concentration.

He stared through the flames as if focused on something, or someone. Then he dropped some dried herbs onto the fire, and the flames leapt higher. And the smoke wafting from the fire turned fragrant with a bittersweet aroma Olivia could not name because she had never smelled anything like it before.

The land had legends of its own about the plants and flowers that grew wild here but nowhere else. The plants and flowers were supposed to be able to cure every ailment but death. And if someone tried to administer the cures and did not understand or appreciate the powers of the plants, they could cause death.

She had never met anyone like Damien's cousin before, either. Not even her mother was as unusual as the shaman. At their first meeting, she had realized that Nathan Gray did not like her. She suspected he had disliked her before they'd even met and had even admitted his antipathy toward her to Damien since her groom had insisted that they marry at city hall instead of the shore of the Lake of Tears with the shaman officiating.

Because of old prejudice or loyalty to Damien's first wife, she had never determined which fueled the shaman's dislike of her.

So would he help her if he could?

"Nathan!" she raised her voice as she called his name again.

But his head didn't lift as he concentrated on the

herbs, dropping more onto the fire. Again the flames leapt, crackling and hissing. And the aroma grew stronger, sweeter and thicker than mere smoke.

"Nathan!"

He stared again at the fire. Was he meditating? Or was there actually someone there, someone he could see and she couldn't?

But she was the spirit, not him. Shouldn't she able to see whatever he could, unless what he saw was only inside his head? "Nathan, please, please, look at me," she pleaded. "I need your help. I need to know…"

The truth about his cousin, her husband. Was he a killer? Many people had warned her that he was. But only one man, besides Damien Gray himself, would know for certain if she had married a killer.

"Nathan, please…"

But he stared at the fire as if in a trance. Desperate to get his attention, Olivia braced herself and stepped inside the flames. Although the fire did not scorch her ghostly body, the heat infused her, warming her. She wasn't entirely dead. She could still feel….

Like the flames leapt with the herbs, she leapt free of the fire—unwilling to risk more pain. That was why she hesitated before lifting her arm and reaching out to him. But her hand, nearly transparent now as her energy ebbed, slipped right through his shoulder. She hadn't so much as nudged him.

Tears of frustration burned her eyes, like the smoke from the fire. Why couldn't he see her?

If he were really a shaman, wouldn't he be able to at least sense her presence as Damien had at the house? But Damien had been able to do more than sense her. Last night he had seen her and felt her.

Her last hope for help flickered like the flames, then snuffed out. "You're a fraud," she murmured.

When she had first heard about Nathan, when the townspeople had talked about him in Grayson, she had doubted his authenticity. She had known other people who claimed supernatural gifts: a college roommate who'd read Tarot cards, an ex-fiancé who relied on his sixth sense as much as his investigative skills to do his police work and a mother who had sworn she was psychic. Olivia hadn't believed any of them—until her death. Now she realized anything was possible.

If he truly had the special abilities he was rumored to have, perhaps he was just ignoring her, hoping she would go away. But she couldn't go, not without pleading with him one last time. "Nathan, please, I need your help. I need…"

She needed to know what the hell the shaman was

doing as he ground a root into powder and sprinkled the powder into a metal flask.

"What is that, Nathan?"

One of his magic potions for which the townspeople praised and revered him? Or something else, something far more sinister? Poison?

And for whom?

Perhaps she was not the only one trying to kill Damien Gray?

Damien stalked into the house, slamming the door behind him with such force that the crystal chandelier rattled. It wasn't just her mother who believed he was a murderer. He suspected that Olivia had tried to kill him the night before because she believed it, too.

He closed his eyes, remembering the hatred burning in hers. Clearly she had wanted revenge last night. His life for hers?

With her gone, he didn't have much of a life anymore. Taking it would give her an empty victory.

He walked into the den, grabbed a drink from the bar and then settled into the leather chair behind his desk. Gulping his drink, he studied the papers atop the mahogany surface. The hair lifted on the nape of his neck as he realized that someone had rifled through them.

Someone had been in the house. Olivia's mother? He hadn't seen her inside, only flitting around outside as if looking through the windows to spy on him. But earlier, he had felt Olivia's presence inside—in the bathroom with him.

Maybe it hadn't been just his imagination. So what had she been looking for? And had she found it?

He picked up the search warrant, which he had been served nearly six months ago. The sheriff hadn't found what he'd been looking for—evidence and Olivia.

Damien swallowed another gulp of Scotch, which warmed his throat and lightened his head. Damn, he had never had alcohol affect him so quickly. Usually it didn't affect him at all. But then he hadn't had a drink in a long while, afraid that if he'd started drinking he might not have stopped. Like Olivia had drowned in the lake, he would have tried drowning himself in alcohol.

But he hadn't had much yet, not enough to affect him as it had. Maybe all the sleepless nights and stress had finally caught up with him.

Ignoring the rearranged papers, he stood up, and his head swam, black spots dancing through his field of vision. He staggered up the steps to the second-story bedroom. And as he fell onto the floor, it occurred to him that he had probably been poisoned.

Olivia? Trying to kill him again?

Chapter 5

Olivia stared up at the house on the hill, only the outlines of the gables and turret visible and that ornate railing of the widow's walk on the rooftop—empty now as it always was, the door to the stairs leading to the roof always locked.

Every window of the Victorian was dark. Usually Damien turned on the lights by now. Usually he stood at the bedroom window staring down at the lake. Looking for her?

Where was he?

Had she scared him away by trying to drown him

the night before? She shook her head, doubting it. Damien Gray wasn't the kind of man to back down from a fight.

Like the lake, Damien was a legend: an intimidating, dangerous man who lived life by his own rules. She remembered their first meeting—his standing on the rocky shore, more handsome than any man she had ever met, his face unreadable as he had declared, *"My land. My law."*

She hadn't wanted to meet him the way she had that day, because she had already had an appointment arranged to meet him the following day, at the casino, for an interview. She had applied for the recently vacated position of the casino's legal counsel.

After skinny-dipping—after *sleeping* with him— she should have canceled the appointment. But she had gone to the casino in Grayson, her knees shaking as she walked to his private office. Following his secretary's direction to walk right in, she had pushed open the door, then been pushed up against the wall—trapped between mahogany paneling at her back and tense, angry male at her front.

"So this was your game yesterday," he said, his deep voice a throaty, threatening growl. "You were *playing* me."

She shook her head.

He arched a dark brow. "So you didn't think you were sleeping your way into a job?"

Pride and anger had her lifting her chin. "I didn't *want* to sleep with you."

His big hand gripped her jaw, holding her face still so that she could not escape the intensity of his glare. "So I forced you?"

"You seduced me."

He chuckled…then he proceeded to seduce her again, right against the wall of his office. While he lowered his head and pressed his mouth to hers, his hands moved. One skimmed over her hip to the hem of her skirt; his fingers trailed up her thigh, caressing, teasing….

The other teased, too, cupping her breast beneath her unbuttoned jacket, his thumb finding her nipple through the silk and lace and stroking it to an aching peak. She moaned into his mouth, as his lips devoured hers in open, biting kisses. The man didn't just kiss—he consumed.

And Olivia, weak with passion, didn't care if he left nothing of her. She had never felt like he made her feel—out of control and giddy with the sense of abandon. She lifted her hands, tangling her fingers in his thick, soft hair—pulling it free of the leather thong that bound the silky black mane at the base of his neck.

"Damien," she murmured, awed, as she had been the day before by his masculine beauty.

He slid his tongue into her open mouth, tangling it with hers in a sensual duel for dominance. A duel in which she quickly conceded his victory.

His hand moved from her breast, as he tugged the buttons free and parted her silk blouse. He unclasped the front closure of her bra, so that the lace cups fell away, baring her to his hungry gaze. Then he lowered his head and closed his lips around her hardened nipple. As he tugged, she felt the pull of desire throughout her trembling body.

Unbearable pressure built inside her, and she tried squeezing her legs together where the ache was most intense. But he moved his hand there, pushing aside the elastic of her panties. He stroked through her curls and slid a finger inside her. She arched her back against the wall and her breast against his mouth, her hands clutching his head to her. "Damien!"

Pleasure jolted her as she came…so easily and quickly for him. Only for him.

He lifted his mouth from her breast, his eyes burning with desire. "You're ready for me…."

A shiver coursed through her at his words and the intensity of his gaze. She wasn't ready for him—not for the feelings overwhelming her. While there was freedom in abandon, there was also fear.

But he tore her panties aside and pushed up her skirt, wrapping her legs around his waist and lifting her against the wall. After unzipping his slacks, his erection pushed inside her, sliding deep. The cords stood out on his neck as he groaned. "Olivia…"

She tensed, recognizing that nothing separated him from her. No protection. Like the day before—when they had made love in the cool water of the Lake of Tears. But then he moved, stroking her core—driving in and out. And like before, like _always_ with him, all rational thought fled her mind.

She could only match his thrusts with an arch of her hips. Burrowing her head in his shoulder, she bit at the cords in his neck—as he reached between them and skimmed his fingers over her nipple, stroking the point to an ache. Then he moved his hand lower, to where his body joined hers, and he rubbed his thumb against the most sensitive part of her.

She wriggled, the pressure winding tighter than before—then breaking loose as an intense orgasm slammed through her. To hold in a scream of pleasure, she bit his neck harder.

He kept thrusting inside her, and she came again—before he joined her—a groan tearing through his clenched teeth, as his penis pulsed, pouring his seed inside her.

Olivia closed her eyes, trying to shut out the memory. But despite the cold spring wind whipping across the lake, heat flashed through Olivia, as it had when she had stood in the flames of the shaman's fire. Just the memory of Damien's mouth, his hands, his body fired her insatiable desire for him. She had never had as thorough a lover. And now she would never have another….

Her life was over.

Because of him? She was beginning to have doubts now. But maybe he had seduced her again, robbing her of her control and common sense, with just the memory of their lovemaking. He was that powerful, that dangerous.

But where was he?

She hadn't heard his car drive away. And she doubted he was asleep already. He had never required much sleep when they were together, as he had awakened her often in the night to make love. And he had seemed to sleep even less after her death, as he endlessly paced in front of the windows. But she caught no glimpse of his shadow moving behind the glass, as she studied the dark windows now.

Another memory flashed through her mind, of the

shaman sprinkling powder into a flask. One of his healing potions? Or poison?

But Nathan would not hurt Damien; he had seemed so protective of his cousin, which she had thought misplaced. She had never considered that Damien might need protection…until now.

The same instinct that had alerted her to danger too late that night on the beach, the night she had died, nagged at her now, adding to her restlessness. Why should she care if something had happened to Damien? Just because the house was dark didn't mean anything was wrong.

But yet her restlessness grew, the foreboding so strong that it drew her from the shore of the lake toward the house. She had to know…if he was all right. She had to know….

Hoping she had not reacted too late again, Olivia hurried up the rocky hill to the house and pushed open the door that was always unlocked. In the dark, she searched the first floor, catching sight of a glass tipped over on his desk, the amber liquid spilled across the papers through which she'd rifled earlier that day. And the sense of foreboding grew, pressing down on her.

"Damien!" Her scream echoed from the high ceiling. But nobody stirred, no one answered her.

She ran up the winding staircase to the second story and the bedroom in which she had spent her honeymoon with her new groom. Until the honeymoon had been cut short with her murder. Her hand trembling, she pushed open the door, which had been left ajar.

The faint glow of a crescent moon dimly illuminated the room—and the man lying on the floor, as if he hadn't been able to make it to the bed.

They had been that way many times—too impatient for each other to make it to the bed. But Damien lay alone on the floor, either too tired or too weak to have made it those last few steps.

Or too dead?

She waited for the flood of relief or vindication, but only fear gripped her. He couldn't be…

She dropped onto the floor beside him, trying to discern if he was breathing. But he lay facedown on the plush rug beside the bed. She couldn't check his chest for movement, or his mouth for air.

God, she was such a fool to care. *How* could she still care about him?

"Damien?" she whispered.

She reached out, brushing her fingers through the soft strands of his dark hair like she had done so many times before. The hair poured over his face and shoulders like black silk. Her hand trembling, she pushed it back, revealing his powerful profile. His skin looked eerily pale in the glow of moonlight, nearly as pale as her hand stroking his face.

Her hand did not pass through him, as it had his cousin. And she could feel Damien, whereas she had not felt Nathan at all.

But Damien did not move. Did he not feel her touch? Because she was dead or because *he* was?

Emotions crashed over her, conflicting feelings of hate and love tearing her apart. *Was he dead?*

"Damien?"

She trailed her fingers along the strong line of his jaw to his neck, to check for a pulse. But before she could locate the telltale beat, a big hand grabbed hers.

He turned his head, staring up at her with dark eyes full of anger and accusation. As though she still had blood flowing through her that could turn cold, Olivia shivered.

He was alive. And he was *mad*.

Damien summoned his strength to tighten his fingers around her hand. He couldn't feel the silkiness of her skin, but he felt the electricity of her touch, the energy of her spirit. He blinked back the waves of black that threatened to pull him under consciousness.

"You tried again," he murmured, fighting to clear his vision and his mind. Fighting to control his reaction to her, which despite everything, was instant and powerful.

"Tried again?" she asked, her soft voice exactly the same as the woman he had known, the woman he had loved. The woman who had now tried to kill him. Not once but twice.

"You tried to kill me," he said, his voice raspy with emotion and weakness. Not from whatever had been slipped into his bottle of Scotch but from seeing her. He resisted the urge to stroke his hand over hers, to entwine their fingers as he often had. He couldn't trust her. He couldn't love her anymore, but his heart had yet to realize that.

She stammered, "I—I didn't—"

"I felt you in the lake, holding me underwater," he accused her, reminding her and himself of her betrayal. "And I saw your face…." Before he had lost consciousness, which threatened again as her image blurred before his eyes. Once again her face would be the last thing he saw—before death tried to claim him.

"I was in the lake," she admitted, and the resentment replaced the bit of concern he'd thought he had glimpsed in her blue eyes when he had first awakened to her hand moving along his jaw and down his throat. "I've been in the lake for six months."

"Except when you're haunting me, walking the

shore—taunting me…" Fighting against the dizziness swimming in his head, he clutched her hand tighter. "I didn't know if it was just my mind playing tricks on me. Now I know it was you…." Anger hardened his voice, strengthening it and him. "*Playing me…*"

Like she had played him before, making him fall in love with her even though he had vowed to never love again after Melanie's senseless death. God, he had been such a fool to risk his heart again. To risk his life…

Like he had always explained when people, even Olivia, had questioned his running of the casinos and had implied that he might be callous or heartless— a person shouldn't gamble what they couldn't afford to lose. It wasn't his fault when people did, and as Olivia had once accused him, he profited from their misfortune. But *this*…this was his fault; he had gambled more than he could afford to lose. His heart. And his life.

"Why, Olivia?" he asked, needing to understand her motives—needing to know how big a fool he'd been. "Why do you hate me so much?"

She stared down at him, those eerily light eyes narrowing with confusion and concern. "Damien…"

"I thought I was losing my mind," he admitted. "I kept seeing you, but yet it wasn't you…." She had never been as solid to him as she was now—as substantial. Not even last night in the water.

"But driving me crazy wasn't enough for you," he said, her betrayal muddling his mind as much as the drugs she must have slipped into his Scotch, "you want to kill me, too."

And as he succumbed to oblivion again, his last thought was that this time she would succeed.

That was what Olivia had thought she wanted: his life—for hers. But she realized now that his dying would bring her more turmoil than peace.

"Come on, Damien," she urged him. "Wake up…."

But his fingers loosened his hold on her, and his hand dropped, limply, back to the hardwood floor next to his still body. His eyes closed, not a lash flickered. Nor did a breath stir a single strand of hair as the thick mane slid across his face again.

Panic welled up in her. "Damien!"

Knowing now that he could feel her, she reached for his shoulders, shaking him. Then she lifted her palm, swinging it toward his face, but he caught her wrist before she could slap him. Relief eased the tightness gripping her. She had known he was too much a fighter to succumb easily to death.

"Thank God…." she murmured. "You're still conscious…." Still alive.

"Isn't this what you want?" Damien asked her, his voice low with the deep timbre of his trademark growl. "My death?"

Yes, this was what she had thought she wanted—what had been driving her past the grief and despair that would have paralyzed her. *Revenge.*

"No," she said, shaking her head as she realized she spoke the truth to him now and had been lying to herself before. "This isn't what I want." Not like this.

She had to get him help. But who? The shaman, who hadn't been able to see her, and who might have been the one who'd poisoned Damien?

And it wasn't like she could just call 911. But *he* could. "Damien, you have to call for help," she urged him. "You have to call the police."

His lips lifted in a faint grin. "The sheriff? He hates me as much as you must…."

"I don't hate you," she said, the words falling out of their own volition. "But I should…"

"You want to hate me," he murmured, as astute as ever. "I want to hate you, too." Somehow he summoned the strength to roll onto his back and pull her down so that she fell across his chest.

The heat of his body scorched her more than the flames of the shaman's fire. She tingled, as if electrically charged, everywhere they touched. Perhaps

Damien was the real shaman, not his cousin, and he had put a spell on her. So that she could not resist him, no matter how much she wanted to…

He lifted the hand, not manacling her wrist, to her hair and brushed it back from her face like she had brushed his back. "But I can't hate you, either," he admitted, his eyes glowing with desire as his gaze moved over the image of her body, in the lace gown she had worn the first night she had been his bride. "I can only *want* you…."

And even dead—even suspecting him responsible for her death—she wanted him. Desire pulsed to life in her body, making her feel alive. Was she that weak? That stupid, when she had always been proud of her intelligence?

"Right now I just want to get you help." She tugged free of his weakening grip and reached for the phone on a table against the wall and pulled it down next to him. "Call 911…."

He shook his head, his jaw clenched. "No. I don't want to…"

"You don't want to die," she assured him. "You don't want to be like me…." Trapped between worlds.

"No, I don't want *you* to go…." He moved his hand from her hair to stroke a finger along her cheek. "You're so real now…even more real than last night…."

Because he was close to death, too? Olivia was afraid that that was how it worked, how he was able to see her and no one else could.

"You have to call for help," she insisted. "I'll still be here…."

Without her revenge—without her justice—she doubted she would ever find the peace that would let her leave the Lake of Tears.

"Don't go," he murmured, his hand dropping away from her face to fall back to his side.

How could he want her with him after what she had done the night before, after she had tried to kill him? Was he that forgiving or that guilty?

"Tell me," he said, his voice a soft growl. "Tell me why you tried to kill me? I have to know…."

"You know," she insisted. "You have to *know*…."

Because if he hadn't killed her, then she had been wrong…so wrong…in trying to kill him.

His dark eyes glazed with pain and confusion, and he stared up at her. "Know? Know what?"

She opened her mouth, ready to pour out all her accusations. All her resentment. But he looked so weak, as if he were barely hanging on to life. "Damien, you have to call for help!"

But he didn't move, and his eyes flickered closed again. Desperate to help him, she summoned all her energy and pushed the buttons on the cordless phone.

A voice emanated from the receiver, "Grayson emergency operator, how can I help you?"

"Send help!" Olivia yelled even though she feared they could not hear her. That was why Damien had needed to call.

"Is there anyone there?" the operator asked.

Olivia glanced down at Damien's unconscious body—and she wondered: was there anyone there? Or had she waited too long to get him help?

Chapter 6

Damien leaned his forehead against the cool glass of the rounded window of the turret and stared out at the fog-enshrouded lake.

"The paramedics said you refused to go to the hospital with them," a gruff male voice commented.

Damien expelled a breath and turned away from the window and the lake. Olivia wasn't down there. Had she been *here?* Really been here or had the vision of her been drug induced from whatever had been slipped into his bottle of Scotch?

He almost wished her appearance had been only

a figment of his imagination. Otherwise he had wasted an opportunity to talk to her and to find out the details of what had happened to her. Had she killed herself as Melanie had? Or had someone killed her, like her mother had witnessed in her vision? Had she been struck over the head and drowned in the Lake of Tears?

Did she blame him, like he blamed himself for not being there for her that night? Or did she blame him because she actually believed he had been the one to kill her?

"Gray, did you hear me?" the sheriff asked, his voice rough with impatience and resentment. "The paramedics said you refused to go with them."

"There's no reason for me to go to the hospital," he said, scoffing at the thought that the sheriff might actually be concerned about his health. "I'm fine."

"*They* say otherwise." Sheriff Matthew Haynes snorted his derision. "But then again, I'm used to you lying to me…."

"The polygraph I took says otherwise," Damien reminded the bitter lawman.

"I have my theory about how you passed that," the sheriff mused, leaning against the doorjamb, as if he were physically unable to fully enter the room that Damien had shared with the man's ex-fiancée. "I figure that in order to react to the questions, a person has to have a conscience. And since you didn't react to a single damn question…"

Years of gambling had taught Damien to control his emotions and any telltale physical reactions of a bluff. Even if he had been guilty, he would have probably passed the test. Not because he didn't have a conscience, as the sheriff thought, but because Damien had control. Around anyone but Olivia…

He had never been able to control his emotions around her, whether she was alive…or dead…

"I thought the rumors about you were true," Sheriff Haynes continued, his voice thick with disgust. "That you're so cold-blooded you're not quite human."

"And something's changed your mind?" Damien asked, with surprise.

The guy had hated him from the first moment they'd met—when Damien had tossed him out of the casino in Grayson for hassling Olivia. Then the son of a bitch, with ancestral roots of his own in Grayson, had talked the city council into hiring him for the position of sheriff that had been vacant for years. Hell, they hadn't even had a uniform to supply the guy; he wore khakis and pinned his badge to the pocket of his denim shirt.

"You changed my mind tonight," the sheriff admitted. "With this…" He gestured toward where the paramedics had left an IV bag and other emergency medical paraphernalia lying on the floor next to the cordless phone.

Damien couldn't remember calling for help. He could only remember her, her fingers stroking through his hair, over his face….

His head pounded, still foggy despite the paramedics having pumped his stomach and administered an IV to counteract the effects of whatever drug he had been given. Could he have imagined everything? Her appearance, her touch?

"Maybe you actually have a conscience after all," the other man commented with the hint of a satisfied grin.

"You think I tried to kill myself?"

Obviously the guy hadn't paid that much attention to all the rumors about Damien, or he would know him…at least the little that everyone else knew about him. Damien Gray had too much pride and honor to take the easy way out of anything, even life.

"The paramedics can't say for sure yet what you took," Sheriff Haynes said. "But the blood sample they got from you is going off to the lab. So is the glass from your den."

"You should have had them take the Scotch bottle, too," Damien advised.

The sheriff's brow furrowed. "So you're claiming someone tried to kill you?"

Damien had thought *she* had. But why then had she helped him—if she truly wanted him dead? He shrugged. "I don't know. It would be easy enough for someone to get in this house."

Remembering the rearranged papers on his desk, he had no doubt that someone had been in his den while he had been out walking in the woods and along the rocky shore of the lake, looking for Olivia.

"Hell, *you've* been in this house a lot over the past six months," Damien recalled, studying the guy through narrowed eyes.

Sheriff Matthew Haynes wasn't a particularly big man—his build more lean than muscular. Yet he had the ego and confidence of a more powerful man. Despite his not being completely unattractive, with dark blond hair and green eyes, Damien had struggled to understand what Olivia had ever seen in the younger man.

But Haynes was probably Olivia's Melanie—her college sweetheart, the one who had been more familiar comfort than love of her life. Until the other day, Damien had thought *he* was the love of her life.

The sheriff bristled with offended pride. "What are you saying? You're accusing *me* of poisoning you?"

Damien lifted a brow. "Like I said, you've been in and out of this house, with your search warrants and your interrogations. You could have slipped something in that bottle in the den at any time."

Because until tonight Damien hadn't been tempted to medicate himself with alcohol. Because he'd worried that if he'd started drinking, he wouldn't stop.

"And why would I do that?" the sheriff asked, his voice hard with resentment.

"You hate my guts," Damien replied matter-of-factly. He didn't care what the guy thought of him. He only cared about Olivia.

"I hate what you *did,*" Sheriff Haynes clarified, "to *her.*"

"You hated me before anything happened to Olivia," Damien reminded him. "You hated me because she loved me like she never loved you."

The sheriff clenched his fists at his sides. "Even though she claimed she knew you, she never really did. She had no idea what kind of man you are."

"But you tried to tell her," he surmised. Even though Olivia had never admitted it, Damien had suspected that the sheriff had been bad-mouthing him. Trying to warn her away from Damien, like her mother had with her "vision." "You tried to turn her against me."

"She wouldn't listen to me," the sheriff admitted, shaking his head at what he must have considered her obstinacy. "She'd bought your lies about how your first wife died."

"I never lied to Olivia." Although it had been painful to admit, he had told her the truth about Melanie, about how his first wife had chosen death over life with him. But Olivia had still accepted his proposal and agreed to be his bride.

"Maybe you've told your lies so many times that you believe them now," Haynes mused with a shrug. "Maybe that's how you passed the polygraph."

"I answered honestly," Damien insisted. "That's how I passed."

The sheriff snorted again. "You're a con artist, Gray. You've made your fortune cheating people out of their hard-earned money. Olivia should have known better than to listen to a man like you."

Although his pride stung at the sheriff's assessment of his character, Damien refused to let the guy goad him into losing control. Instead he goaded the sheriff. "She should have listened to *you?* The man who'd been too obsessed to accept her rejection even after she married another man?"

"The man she'd known longer. The man she'd loved and trusted until *you* manipulated her," Haynes said, his voice shaking with anger and resentment. He brushed a trembling hand over his military-style short blond hair. "Until it was too late, she never knew what you were capable of."

Damien shook his head. "I think it was *you* she underestimated."

And maybe Damien had, too. Matthew Haynes had been so obsessed with Olivia that he had followed her to Grayson even after she'd broken their engagement. Had he been so obsessed that—not wanting another man to have her if he couldn't—he had killed her?

Instead of anger, Damien actually felt a surge of relief. These past six months he had believed Olivia had killed herself—that, like Melanie, she had chosen death over life with him. But then the relief evaporated and the anger rushed back, threatening his control.

"If I find out you hurt her—that you *killed* her, you're going to wish you were dead," he promised Haynes.

"You're threatening me?" the sheriff asked as tense as if bracing himself for a fight.

Knowing the lawman had been looking for any excuse to arrest him, Damien shook his head. "Nope.

Just reminding you of your own advice. You have *no* idea what I'm capable of."

But if Haynes was responsible for Olivia's death, they would both find out….

"He's a goddamn son of a bitch," Matthew Haynes hurled the curse across the surface of the lake like Damien had thrown the roses. "Why, Olivia? Why *him?*"

The moon, nearly full now, glowed bright enough to shine through the fog. And she stood beside him, but like Nathan, Matt could not see her. Only Damien could.

"Why not *me?*" he asked, his deep voice breaking with the pain of her rejection.

She reached out, touching his arm, trying to offer him comfort as tears shimmered in his green eyes. But her fingers passed through him; he could not feel her. Only Damien could.

But her connection with Damien had always been deeper than her connection with Matt despite all the years she and her ex-fiancé had known each other.

"I'm sorry," she murmured. "So sorry…"

She hadn't wanted to hurt him. She suspected that was why she had accepted his proposal in the first place—because she hadn't known how to tell him no and explain that they hadn't had enough between them on which to build a marriage.

"But maybe I should have married you anyways," she said. "You wouldn't have hurt me…." Because she wouldn't have been as emotionally involved, as vulnerable, as she had been with Damien. "I never should have listened to my mother…." And her bizarre warning that Olivia's husband would kill her.

But Olivia had only listened; she really hadn't believed. She had grown up with her father calling Ana Olsson a crazy, unstable woman. So he had convinced her that she shouldn't believe anything her mother claimed. But even though she hadn't believed her, Olivia had used her mother's vision as an excuse to return the ring she had never really been comfortable wearing.

And, in her haste to marry Damien, she had forgotten the warning. It wasn't until after her death that she had truly accepted that her mother had been right.

Matt had tried to warn her, too, when he'd moved to Grayson and accepted the position of sheriff to the town, which would have been small and rural if not for the presence of Damien Gray's flagship Gray Wolf Casino—and the hotels, condos and restaurants that had been built and prospered in the town because of the casino. Because of him. Even more than his cousin, the shaman, Damien Gray was revered, idolized and *feared* in Grayson.

Because Matt had ties to the town, too, through his mother, whose ancestors had belonged to the same tribe as the original Gray Wolf, the townspeople had accepted him. And confided in him.

Olivia shivered as she remembered his warning. He'd come to the casino, to the office from which Damien had physically thrown him the week before. *Her* office, since Damien had hired her for the position of the casino's legal counsel.

"Olivia, you have to get away from this guy," Matt warned. "He's dangerous."

The bruise around his eye had faded from purple to yellow, and Olivia hadn't argued with him. Damien Gray was not a man a person would be wise to cross. Or anger.

Or maybe to love. But it had been too late for her, then. She had already fallen harder and faster than she had ever believed she could fall.

"Matt…" She had struggled with old feelings for him, of friendship and regret. But not love. She knew now that she had never really loved him…like she loved Damien.

"I know you think I'm jealous," he said then admitted, "I am. But I'm also telling you the truth. Damien Gray is a dangerous man. He killed his first wife."

She shook her head. "No, she killed herself." And Damien still suffered, blaming himself for the tragedy.

"That's what he wanted everyone to believe," Matt said. "But he's the one who threw her off the roof of the house onto the rocks below. She did not jump."

Olivia closed her eyes to the horrific image Damien had discovered, when he had come home to find his wife dead—her broken body smashed against the boulders on the rocky shore. "No. He wasn't even there when she died." He had found her the following morning.

"He has no alibi," Matt persisted.

"He was here, at the casino."

"Alone in his office. No one can prove that he didn't go out his private door," the lawman went on, "that he didn't go home and kill her then come back."

"No one can prove that he did," she pointed out.

"Not yet," Matt agreed, sticking out his chest where the badge glinted on his shirt pocket. "But I will."

"Why, Matt?" she asked, suspecting his motives more than she'd suspected he might actually be right about the man she loved.

"Because he's guilty," Matt insisted.

"Not of murder," she said, confident then in Damien's innocence and his love. "He's only guilty of stealing my heart."

"From me," Matt added, his eyes hard with bitterness.

She could have corrected him. Damien hadn't been able to steal from Matt what he had never really had. "Don't open up his pain over his past because you're jealous. You're a better man than that."

"I'm a better man than he is," Matt claimed. "I would never hurt you, Olivia. But *he* will."

Had Matt been right? She hadn't thought so at the time. But now…

Matt squeezed his eyes shut and fisted his hands at his sides. "He should have died. The son of a bitch should have died tonight…."

Cold penetrated Olivia as deeply as the icy water in which she'd drowned. Could Matt have been responsible…could he have tried to kill Damien?

"You shouldn't be investigating this," she told her ex-fiancé, wishing he could hear her. "You have a personal stake in all of this—" her murder, the attempt on Damien's life "—unless you don't care about me anymore…."

But from the tears shimmering in his green eyes, she knew he still cared. Maybe too much.

Perhaps she wasn't the only one who wanted revenge against Damien. But did Matt want it because he believed Damien had killed her or because he knew she had loved Damien far more than she had ever loved him?

"You need to leave Grayson," she said. But she had told him that when he had been able to hear her. He hadn't listened then, and she doubted he would listen now. "You need to let me go…."

She wanted Matt to let her go, but she wasn't sure about Damien. He was the only one who could see her, who could feel her….

Glancing up at the house, she glimpsed a shadow moving behind the curved glass of the bedroom window. Even though Damien was better, no relief eased the tension gripping her.

She had that uneasy feeling again—that prickly premonition of imminent danger. And she suspected that someone else was going to wind up dead.

The Wise One stared out over the lake, hatred charging his energy, fueling his power. Finally, after centuries of frustration, he was close to achieving his goal. The Gray Wolf warrior had nearly died tonight. And with his death, the woman would be released from this world.

Did she know that? Was that why she had saved the warrior? To save herself? The Wise One hoped she had acted out of self-preservation. And not love.

Love had conquered him once. He would not allow it to beat him again. No, he had a plan. And the Gray Wolf warrior had to die in order to ensure the success of the ancient shaman's plan. Tonight was just the first attempt. There would be more…until Damien Gray died.

Then the Wise One would not have to share this ghostly realm—or his power—with anyone.

Soon.

Chapter 7

Damien lifted his face toward the heat of the flames as he settled onto the ground beside his cousin. Nathan, in one of his trances, didn't even notice his presence. Damien wished he could lose himself in meditation, too—that he could leave this world and the weight of his guilt and grief—for just a little while. But he couldn't, not even when he had been so close to death the other night.

He stared into the flames, acknowledging that he didn't need to go to hell to live it. Hell wasn't fire. Hell was living without Olivia....

"Do you see him?" Nathan asked, his voice querulous with awe and excitement.

"Who?"

"The ancient shaman," Nathan said softly, as if not wanting to scare away the apparition.

Ordinarily Damien would have discounted his cousin's claim of the ghostly apparition. But after seeing Olivia…

"Is this the kid, the son of the shaman that called himself the Wise One?" As he recalled the legend, the kid was the real wise one, the one who had understood that a true shaman cared only about healing— both physically and spiritually. Cared so much in fact that Nathan claimed the boy had come back from the dead to serve as his guide. "Where is he?"

Nathan pointed a shaking finger toward the fire. "He dances inside the circle of flames."

Damien narrowed his eyes and concentrated, but he saw only the smoke, his eyes stinging from the thick, pungent haze of it. "I can't see him."

"But you can see *her?*" Nathan asked, as if disgusted with his cousin's inability to see what he considered important, an ancient ghost.

"I can't even see her anymore," he admitted. Not since the night she had saved him.

"She's gone?" His cousin turned toward him, giving Damien his full attention.

He shrugged. "I don't think so." Because even though he couldn't see her, he could still *feel* that she was near. Somewhere…

"You don't think she's found peace yet?"

"No." Because he could feel her restlessness, too, as if it coursed through his body with the blood pumping through his veins. Like passion for her had coursed through him. Even when he'd hovered on the verge of death, he had wanted her.

He'd needed her….

As desperately as he had needed her when they had first met that day on the shore of the Lake of Tears. Ever since Melanie's suicide, guilt and grief had held Damien somewhere between life and death. He had concentrated on running the casinos, on doing the work he knew and could control. He had given no time or consideration to his personal life, resolved to never love again.

But like Anya had resurrected the fearless warrior Gray Wolf all those centuries ago, Olivia had resurrected Damien…with her touch. Her fingertips had skimmed his bare chest as she had lifted her mouth to his. And with her kiss…she'd breathed life—*love*—back into him.

"Thank you," she murmured, as she pulled back.

"For what?" he asked, jarred by another shock of recognition, of this woman's lips, of her kiss. He'd realized then that *she* was *his* destiny.

"Thank you," she said, "for telling me the legend of the lake…."

"Why are you interested?" he wondered, touching her face, his fingertips gliding across her skin as hers glided yet across his, over the muscles of his bare chest.

Her pupils dilated, the black swallowing the pale blue. "I'm interested…"

"In the lake," he prodded her as her thought trailed off. He fought a smile from curving his lips, his ego boosted by the blatant desire in her eyes.

"In the lake…I'm interested in the lake—" her delicate throat moved as she swallowed—"because I've been told I look like the woman."

"Anya," he said. "She was described as having hair the color of moonlight and eyes like chips of a pale-blue sky…."

A smile tugged up her full lips. "But *she* was powerful. She brought back her warrior from the dead."

Damien discounted the supernatural ability of the ancient woman. "She was powerful because she seduced him into falling for her despite his mission being to kill her."

"But he knew she was no threat to him," Olivia said, as if these people from so many centuries ago were familiar to her, "like the shaman had tried to persuade him and the rest of his people."

"She was only a threat to the shaman."

"Who the warrior killed." Her breath shuddered out. "Even after the shaman had pierced his heart with a spear, the warrior had had enough strength, enough *life,* left to throw a dagger and kill the shaman to protect Anya from the madman."

"He loved her," Damien simply explained his ancestor's action.

"But it was men who'd looked like her—with pale hair and skin—who had killed his first wife," she remembered, almost, what Damien had told her.

"Woman," he corrected her, since his ancestors had not known about nor believed in marriage. Yet they had been more monogamous, more loyal, than today's husbands and wives. "And no, Gray Wolf only thought that when he'd accepted his mission to kill Anya. It came out later, after his death, that the shaman had killed the woman."

"He was evil," she said, shuddering.

Damien shrugged. "He was greedy for power. He wanted *all* the power and complete control of this land."

"That was why he ordered her death," Olivia said.

"Because she was powerful…so powerful she brought her warrior back from the dead."

"You are like her," Damien mused, as his heart shifted against his ribs—reawakening when for so long he had thought it dead. He reached, as he had earlier, for the buttons on her vest.

This time she didn't slap his hand away. She let him undo the buttons and open the linen vest to reveal the wispy lace bra that barely covered the full curves of her breasts and the dusky-rose nipples that puckered with cold…and passion. Her breath catching, she lifted her gaze to his, her eyes wide with confusion and desire.

"I—I shouldn't do this…." she murmured, bemused as if she had never experienced as powerful an attraction before, either.

"You can't truly experience the legend of the Lake of Tears until you swim in its water," he persuaded her, pushing the vest from her shoulders.

Her lips curved into a wide smile. "You just want to see me naked."

He laughed then admitted, "Yes."

As her gaze slid like a caress over his chest, he added, "And you want to see me naked, too."

Her tongue flitted across her bottom lip. "Yes."

He reached for his belt, unclasped it then unzipped

and dropped his jeans and briefs onto the rocky shore. He toed off his shoes and stood naked before her.

Her breath shuddered out again, and she wobbled on her feet, as if overwhelmed. But he didn't touch her again. He turned away and walked into the lake. Moments later water splashed as she joined him, submerging herself to her neck. But he could see her body through the clear, cool water, which had lifted goose bumps on her pale skin.

"You lied. It's cold," she accused him, her teeth clicking together.

"I'll warm you up," he offered, pulling her into his arms. Her wet breasts pressed against his chest, her nipples rubbing across his skin. He groaned at the sensual contact. Their bodies brushed lower, his erection pressing against her stomach.

"You're not cold," she mused, shivering but this time maybe with desire rather than a chill, as she wrapped her legs around his waist.

He wound her wet hair around his fingers, holding her head still for his kiss—as he devoured her sweet mouth, nibbling at her lips and marauding with his tongue. Until she moaned and arched her hips.

Kicking with his legs, he swam them close enough to shore that he could brace his feet on the rock ledge—giving himself more freedom to explore and enjoy her body. He lifted her, until her breasts floated on the surface. Then he lowered his head, sliding his lips from hers, over the curve of her jaw, down her throat, over the delicate curve of her collarbone to the curve of her breast. His mouth covered her nipple, teasing the pebbled point with his teeth and his tongue.

She pushed her fingers into his hair, holding him against her as she moaned, begging for more. "Please…"

Under the water, his fingers found her—tunneling through her blond curls to her slick heat. She was ready for him—more ready than he was for her. But he thought nothing of protection, for her or himself. Instead he lowered her, thrusting inside her. Her muscles tight, she tensed and stared up at him, her eyes wide with awe.

He reached between them, rubbing his thumb against the delicate nub of her sexuality. She wound her arms tight around his shoulders and pressed her body to his, writhing against him as she came.

Blood pounding in his veins like the beat of an ancient war drum, Damien thrust in and out. Driving deep, he connected with her in a way he had never connected with another woman. Olivia had not only claimed his heart that day; she had claimed his soul….

"Damien!" Nathan shouted his name, pulling him from his memories.

"She hasn't found peace," he finally answered his cousin's question, his voice raspy with the emotion memories of her always invoked.

Nathan sighed and warned him, "She may never find peace."

Damien suspected that neither would he. "Why do you think that? About her?" he asked, curious about his insightful cousin's opinion of Olivia.

"She never found peace while she was alive," he said. "She left her family, her job, her fiancé behind in Detroit and moved up here looking for something."

"I thought she found it with me," Damien admitted, knowing he sounded like a romantic fool, a man who had fallen for a woman at first sight.

Nathan, his voice gentle with sympathy, pointed out, "Then she wouldn't have killed herself."

"I'm not so sure anymore that she did."

"But that's what you thought," Nathan reminded him.

"She didn't leave a note." Like Melanie had. "I just figured…" That he had driven a second woman to suicide.

"You said she hadn't been happy," his cousin said, "like a new bride should be on her honeymoon."

There had been times she had seemed happy and secure, when she'd lain naked in his arms after they had made love. And there had been times he had caught her crying, and she hadn't been able to explain her tears.

"I tried to make her happy." But maybe he didn't have the capacity to make a woman completely happy.

"You tried harder with Olivia than you ever had with Melanie," Nathan commented with a trace of resentment.

"I thought I'd learned from my mistakes," he said. "I tried to give more of myself to Olivia. But in the end, she hadn't seemed happy. She was so emotional…." Insecure and weepy. All the things he would have never imagined her to be, but then he hadn't really known her long enough or well enough to make her his bride. But he'd loved her….

"And you've never been comfortable with emotion," Nathan remarked.

So Damien had taken a break from their honeymoon, and Olivia's emotions, to check in on business at the casino in Grayson. And when he'd come back, she was gone—only her velour robe and high-heeled slippers left on the rocky shore of the Lake of Tears.

"I will never forgive myself for leaving her alone that day." Regret and grief tied his stomach into knots. "I should have known what could happen…."

"After Melanie," Nathan murmured. "Have you ever seen *her* ghost?"

"No."

His cousin uttered a sigh of relief. "Then maybe she's at peace."

Or maybe Damien hadn't had the connection with his first wife that he'd had with Olivia. But that connection was broken now. "Nathan, is there something you can give me, something that'll help me see her again?"

"Olivia?"

"Yes. I need to see her," he said, desperation clawing at him. "I need to talk to her." To taste her lips, to touch her body…

"Damien—"

"I need to talk to her," he insisted. "I need to find out what really happened to her."

"You know. You're just struggling to accept it. That's why you need to leave here. Go to one of the other casinos, one of your other houses," the shaman advised.

Damien shook his head, unable to accept his cousin's advice as the townspeople always did.

"Leave," Nathan insisted. "And don't come back."

He shook his head again. "I can't leave her."

"She left you first."

"But I'm not sure that was her choice." Or if

someone, maybe the sheriff, had taken that choice away from her. "You've got all those potions you concoct. You can give me something—"

Nathan sighed. "You don't believe in our heritage, Damien. You don't believe in the powers of the shaman or this sacred land. So I can't help you."

"I believe in *her.* I've seen her. I've talked to her." He dragged in a breath of air, which burned his throat with the thick smoke. "I need to know what really happened to her, or I'm never going to have any peace."

"But maybe knowing the truth will make you feel even worse," Nathan warned him as he tossed herbs onto the fire. Sparks in blue and green sputtered out of the flames. "Maybe it's better that you don't know what happened, what you might have done."

"What are you talking about?" Dread strangled Damien more than the smoke. "Oh, don't tell me you share the sheriff's suspicions? You really think I could have hurt Melanie or Olivia?"

"Maybe not consciously," Nathan allowed.

"What are you saying?" Damien asked, tension cramping his muscles as he waited for his cousin's explanation.

"Because of this land," Nathan gestured around the woods, "because of our heritage, we're capable of doing things that other people are not capable of doing, that they do not have the power to carry out."

The dread pressed on Damien's chest, stealing his breath. "I don't understand…."

"Like the shaman visits me, maybe his father, the Wise One, visits you, too."

"I told you—I can't see anyone but Olivia." And now not even her. Damien had no special ability, no power. If he had, he would bring her back to him.

"But I know he sees *you*," Nathan said, with an almost indiscernible trace of jealousy. "Maybe he possesses you and makes you do things you wouldn't ordinarily do."

Damien snorted with derision, remembering why he had always been unable to believe all the fanciful things Nathan had embraced. "That's crazy."

"Since you've seen her ghost, you must now know that anything's possible."

"No, that's not possible," Damien rejected his cousin's horrific theory. "I couldn't have hurt Olivia. I couldn't have…"

"Like I said," Nathan reminded him, "maybe it's better if you don't know what really happened."

Damien could not believe himself capable of intentionally hurting either Melanie or Olivia. But did Olivia believe he had? Was that why she had tried to kill him in the lake? And why did she believe that? Had he harmed her?

If he had, she should not have let him live....

Olivia studied the door at the bottom of the stairwell that led to the widow's walk on the roof. Unlike the front door, this door was always locked. And when she'd asked, Damien had refused to give her the key. During her search the other day, Olivia hadn't turned up one that looked as though it would fit this antique lock. She hadn't even found a skeleton key. Did Damien carry it on him? Or had he thrown away the key after Melanie's death?

Olivia reached out to rattle the knob, but her fingers passed through the antique brass. Then she lifted her arm, which disappeared through the six-panel mahogany door. Tense and bracing herself for pain, she squeezed her eyes shut and stepped forward—through the door. So, she could pass through walls. Just now, because she'd grown weaker—her image fainter? Was that because she was close to finding peace? Or because she had gone days without seeing Damien, without touching him?

She ached to be with him again. But she needed to learn the truth first, before she could trust him and her feelings for him. Resolved, she climbed the steep steps and passed through the door onto the section of roof that the ornate railing surrounded.

This was where earlier Gray women had watched their husbands and sons out on the lake, where they had assured themselves of the safety of their loved ones. Olivia was not the only one who had lost her life in the Lake of Tears. But the earlier deaths had been accidents, due to the inclement weather or hazards of fishing.

Olivia's death had been no accident.

Had Melanie's?

Instead of looking out at the lake, Olivia peered around the widow's walk. Then she called out, "Melanie? Melanie?"

This was from where Damien's first wife had leapt to her death. From the widow's walk onto the rocky slope of the hill. But had she leapt, or had she been thrown from the roof, from the house, from Damien's life?

Olivia had to know. "Melanie?"

Before her death, Olivia had been able to feel Damien's first wife's presence in the house, in the pretty floral wallpaper in the dining room and the sunny yellow walls of the kitchen. Melanie had been present in the warmth that permeated the house that could have been, due to stature and elegance, austere.

Without ever having met her, Olivia had known that Melanie Gray had been a special woman. And because of that, she had felt threatened.

But the dead woman hadn't been the threat. Someone else had. To both of them?

Olivia gripped the railing of the walk, grateful her hands did not pass through the delicate wood, as the height was dizzying. "Melanie?"

Only sunlight shimmered on the rooftop, no ghostly apparition—besides Olivia herself. Anxious to leave the height of the roof, Olivia passed back through the passage and silently through the house until she stood on the steep slope below. Years of weather had removed blood that might have once stained the rocks where Melanie had fallen. So Olivia could only visually measure the distance and guess where her body had landed.

"Melanie, are you here?" she asked, her desperation growing. She needed to talk to the other woman; she needed to know the truth.

Matt had shared his suspicions—that Damien had thrown his first wife to her death. If he were the man Olivia had briefly suspected he was, the kind of man who valued his freedom more than life, he might have killed Melanie. But if he'd valued his freedom, why had he proposed to Olivia in the first place?

Get 2 Books FREE!

GET 2 BOOKS

We'd like to send you two *Silhouette® Nocturne*™ novels absolutely free. Accepting them puts you under no obligation to purchase any more books.

HOW TO GET YOUR
2 FREE BOOKS AND TWO FREE GIFTS

1. Return the reply card today, and we'll send you two *Silhouette Nocturne* novels, absolutely free! We'll even pay the postage!

2. Accepting free books places you under no obligation to buy anything, ever. Whatever you decide, the free books and gifts are yours to keep, free!

3. We hope that after receiving your free books you'll want to remain a subscriber, but the choice is yours—to continue or cancel, any time at all!

EXTRA BONUS

You'll also get two free mystery gifts! (worth about $10)

FREE!

If offer card is missing, write to Silhouette Reader Service, P.O. Box 1867, Buffalo, NY 14240-1867 or visit www.ReaderService.com

BUSINESS REPLY MAIL

FIRST-CLASS MAIL   PERMIT NO. 717   BUFFALO, NY

POSTAGE WILL BE PAID BY ADDRESSEE

Silhouette Reader Service
PO BOX 1867
BUFFALO NY 14240-9952

NO POSTAGE
NECESSARY
IF MAILED
IN THE
UNITED STATES

And if he had killed for freedom, why did he not enjoy it now instead of staying at the house and the lake as if he were a prisoner of the estate?

"Melanie!" Olivia called again, but nothing appeared on the shore, not even Olivia's shadow. "Why aren't you here?" she asked. "Why am I the only ghost haunting the Lake of Tears?"

A place of so much tragedy had to have left more restless spirits than just hers. Why was Olivia so alone?

"Melanie!" she screamed—futilely. "Why did you find peace and I can't?"

Didn't Melanie Gray want justice? Vengeance? Or was it true what Damien had told her about his first wife, that she had killed herself? And if he hadn't killed Melanie, maybe he hadn't killed Olivia, either.

But if he hadn't, who had? And was that person the same one who had poisoned Damien?

With only the light of the crescent moon penetrating the thick clouds and mist, Damien walked the rocky shore. He brought her no flowers now that he knew she didn't want flowers from him.

He wasn't sure what she wanted from him. He had once thought he'd known—that she'd wanted his heart, his soul. And while he had struggled with opening up himself completely, he had decided to give her everything that he was. But she was already gone when he had come home that night.

But she had returned…if only as a ghost.

"Olivia?" he called to her, calling her back again. "Olivia!"

No one had given him the results yet of the blood work the sheriff had ordered. Maybe more than the alcohol had been poisoned. Maybe his food—despite the little he'd eaten in the past six months? Had the earlier images of her also been drug induced? Had he only imagined her?

He followed the shore to where the water lapped against the rocks. The legs of his faded jeans darkened as the denim soaked up the lake. Mist floated across the dark surface, which barely a ripple disturbed.

"Olivia!"

Thunder rumbled in the distance, echoing his shout. And the clouds shifted, growing dark and dropping lower in the sky. Lightning cracked, and rain began to fall, drops streaking down Damien's face like tears. So used to guarding his emotions, he hadn't even cried when he lost her. She had deserved his tears. God, she had deserved more than he had ever given her.

Focused as he was on the lake, he didn't notice that he was no longer alone—until a dark shadow moved across the surface of the water. Before he could turn to confront whoever had crept up behind him, something slammed into the back of his skull.

Pain exploding inside his head, Damien's world went dark…until water filled his mouth and nose, choking him. He sank beneath the depths of the lake, too disoriented from the blow to remember how to swim, how to fight….

As he sank deep, Damien peered through the rippling water—and he saw her. His bride had come back.

To finish him off?

Chapter 8

The Wise One watched the surface of the water, which was illuminated by a flash of lightning. No bubbles rose or ripples disrupted the glasslike appearance of the lake. Satisfaction lifted his spirit, and he radiated energy.

For the first time in years the water reflected back his image. He wore only a buckskin loincloth, his chest bare but for streaks of a warrior's blood smeared across his dark skin. Blood also smeared his cheekbones, his face as handsome as if carved from stone. The face of a god—one who should have been worshipped, not destroyed.

This time the Gray Wolf warrior would not rise from the lake. This time Damien Gray would die, and unlike the woman—the sorceress—he would stay dead. Because no one had the power to resurrect this warrior. No one was more powerful than the Wise One.

Olivia stared at the shock on Damien's face, at the pain distorting his handsome features. Like before, she felt no vindication in his pain, no sense of triumph. Of course she had had nothing to do with hurting him.

So she should feel no guilt. Yet like before, in the house, she could not let him die. As he sank through the water, she caught him around the waist and kicked, trying to drag him back to the surface. But as he weakened, so did she—her energy fading.

Each time she rose from the icy depths of the lake, she had to fight harder to escape the current of the water, the current that tugged at her, pulling her back under. But she didn't fight just for herself this time; she fought for him. The man she loved.

As she accepted her feelings for Damien—that she still loved him—her energy and her strength increased. She tightened her grasp around his lean waist and pressed her face against his chest. His heart throbbed, in a sluggish beat, beneath her cheek. Despite the tattered skirt of her gown, she stretched her legs in a scissor kick that was powerful enough to propel them to the surface.

Rain fell so hard that the sky was nearly indiscernible from the lake. Olivia swam until Damien's feet dragged against the rocks. Coughing and choking, he gasped for air as he collapsed onto the shore. She glanced around but could see no one—no one to help him and no one who could have hurt him. She'd seen no one but him in the water.

"I'm sorry," he murmured. "So sorry…"

For what was he apologizing? For killing her? Or for trying to kill himself?

"What are you sorry for?" Olivia asked, her voice soft and her eyes watchful.

Damien pushed his lake-and-rain-drenched hair back from his face. "I'm sorry I failed you…."

Her brow furrowed in confusion. "Damien…"

"I wasn't there when you needed me," he said, letting all his guilt and self-loathing pour out like the rain poured from the dark clouds hanging low overhead. "I didn't save you…like you've saved me."

Lightning cracked, and the ground shuddered as a tree fell in the woods. Then flames flickered briefly before the rain doused the fire.

"You have to get to the house," she said, still trying to save him—this time from himself.

Damien surged to his feet, but his legs were leaden and he stumbled, his vision blurring from the pain in his head. "I—I can't make it up the hill," he admitted, although he hated confessing to a weakness. Yet this weakness was nothing in comparison to failing her the only time she had really needed him. To save her.

"Damien, you have to move," she said, her voice high with urgency as thunder boomed. "You're going to get struck by lightning."

He touched the back of his head, where the flesh had swollen and blood oozed across his fingers. "I've already been struck...."

"Oh, my God..." She stared at the blood on his hand, her eyes wide with shock.

"I'm fine," he said, uttering the first lie he'd ever told her. The rain washed away the blood, but still the shock remained on her face. "What? What is it, Olivia?"

She blinked and focused on him, looking as disoriented as Nathan surfacing from a trance. Then she glanced toward the threatening clouds.

"Olivia? Tell me what's wrong," he urged her.

"We can't talk here," she shouted above the sudden boom of thunder. She slid her arm around his waist again, and as if stronger in death than she had been even in life, she managed to help him up the slippery, rock-strewn hill to the house.

When they stumbled through the door, she gasped as the light from the chandelier washed over his face, illuminating the blood that soaked the back of his hair and trailed down the side of his face.

"You have to call for help," she insisted.

"I have help," he said, wrapping his arm tight around her shoulders. "I have *you*."

"I'm not…" she stammered, "I'm not…*real*. No one else can see me or hear me."

"You're real to me," he said, marveling that he could feel her—her heat, her energy—the passion that had been instantaneous and undeniable between them from the moment they had first met. Her breast pushed against his side, the nipple peaked with cold. And desire? "Olivia…"

She lifted her hand to his face, her touch soft as she stroked raindrops and a smear of blood from his cheek. "You need medical assistance, and the police."

Damien snorted his disgust for the sheriff. "Haynes will accuse me of trying to kill myself again."

"Again?"

"He thinks I poisoned myself," he said. "That my guilty conscience made me do it."

"Guilty conscience?" Her voice grew softer yet. "Do you have a guilty conscience?"

"Yes."

When she gasped, he explained, "For not helping you, for not being here when you needed me…"

Her blue eyes warmed. "Damien…"

"But I would *never* hurt you…" No matter what Nathan considered possible, he was incapable of hurting the woman he loved.

Her hand slid from his face, and she eased out from under his arm. Walking away from him, she moved farther into the house, away from the foyer and the light of the sparkling chandelier.

"Matt can't say you hit yourself over the back of the head. You really need to call the police and the paramedics," she insisted. "I don't know why they came last time. They can't hear me."

His legs steady now and the pain and dizziness clearing from his head, he followed her to where she stood at the foot of the stairs. "I'm fine."

And he was now. He had regained his strength— and her.

Olivia shook her head, and her platinum hair, drying from the rain, tumbled around her shoulders. "Someone tried to kill you."

"Again." He stared at her, studying her. "Are you ready to talk now?"

She nodded, knowing it was time.

"Tell me what happened that night," he urged her. "Tell me how you died." His throat moved as he swallowed hard. "And tell me who did it."

"You thought I did," she realized, with surprise and wounded pride. "You thought I killed myself…."

"After Melanie had…that was my first thought," he admitted.

"I wouldn't—*ever*—take my own life." She'd had too much to live for, even more than he knew. She pressed her palm against her flat stomach, grief filling the emptiness that now yawned inside her. She had not been the only one to die that night six months ago.

"I'm sorry," he said. "I should have known…." He sighed. "I should have known *you.*"

"There was so much we didn't know about each other." But she couldn't tell him everything. If he really mourned her, and in her heart she believed he did, she couldn't add to his grief. "Maybe we married too soon."

Damien shook his head. "The only thing that happened too soon was your death. Tell me what happened."

"The same thing that happened to you tonight," she said. "I was waiting for you down on the shore."

Rage flashed in his dark eyes, and he grimaced again. "And someone hit you over the head?"

Pain reverberated in her mind as she relived the blow. "Yes."

"That's what your mother said," he murmured.

"My mother?" She thought first of her step-mom, the woman who had helped her father raise her. But Beverly would have known nothing of the circumstances of her death. Ana Olsson had been the one who'd warned Olivia of her vision. "My mom is *here?*"

He nodded. "I followed her as she left the house the other day and caught up with her in the woods. She described your murder. I didn't believe her."

"I didn't believe her, either," Olivia admitted, "when she first told me about her 'vision.'"

"You two are—were—estranged?"

She shrugged. "I wouldn't call it that. We're more like strangers. Dad and Beverly raised me."

"She said your father took you away from her."

"She had visitation. She just hadn't visited much." Pain flashed through Olivia again, as she remembered her disappointment. Olivia had learned to distance herself, to not care about the woman who'd given birth to her. If Olivia had had the chance, she would have been a much better mother. From Ana she had learned what not to do.

"She told me about her vision," Damien said again, "but I want you to tell me what happened. Because she has some of it wrong. *I* didn't hurt you." His deep voice shaking with passion, he swore, "I would *never* hurt you."

"So many people warned me about you…."

"And you believed them?"

She shook her head. "Not before. But after…I didn't know what to believe anymore…."

"Believe in me," he urged her. "Tell me what happened to you, so we can figure this out together."

"Damien…"

"Please, Olivia, I need to know." A grimace distorted his handsome face.

"You need medical attention." Concern for his well-being grew stronger than her need for justice. Perhaps if she dialed 911 the paramedics would come again, as they had last time even though the dispatcher hadn't heard her.

"I'm fine," he said, dismissing his injury. "Please, tell me while we have this chance."

He was right. She didn't know how long she would be visible to him this time, or if she would ever be visible to him again. And maybe she needed to tell him about that night, to watch his expression for any reaction. For any hint of guilt.

She lifted her chin and continued, "Right before I got hit over the head, I heard your car, coming up the drive to the house."

Color drained from his face. "I was here when it happened?"

"That's partly why I thought it was you," she admitted. The sound of his car and the feeling of his presence when she'd been in the water. "I thought you must have come right down to the lake."

"I didn't. I went to the house first." He pushed a shaky hand through his hair. "But your robe was still warm when I found it on the shore. But all I saw was the robe and your shoes."

Just the robe and her shoes? Not what else she'd brought with her, to show him?

"I must have already been in the lake then," she surmised. "I woke up when I hit the water. It was so cold."

She shuddered now, remembering how the extreme cold of the icy water had burned her skin like flames and how quickly it had constricted her lungs and drowned her.

He reached for her, closing his arms around her trembling body as if to warm her. But she was too cold. "Olivia," he murmured. "Sweetheart…"

"I fought," she insisted. And not just for herself.

"I tried to break free, but someone held me down until I couldn't breathe—until I died…."

Damien released her, abruptly. And after pulling away from her, he slammed his fist through the brocade fabric and the wall behind it. Curses flew from his lips.

"I was *there*," he said, his voice shaking with anger and frustration. "I had to be there. After I found your robe, I jumped in the lake. I kept looking for you, trying to find you."

Was that why she'd felt him, why she had sensed his presence in the lake? It wasn't because it had been his hands holding her under but because he'd been near, trying to find her?

"You're hurt again," she mused, reaching for his hand—the knuckles oozing blood like the wound on his head.

"This physical pain is nothing," he said, "compared to what I'm feeling inside. It *kills* me to know what happened to you, to know that you're *gone*…."

"I'm not gone," she reminded him. "I'm here." But again, she didn't know for how long, or if she would ever be able to come back.

When once she had wanted to cause him pain, now she wanted to ease it. Her fingers gentle on the nape of his neck, she pulled his head down for her kiss. Electricity hummed like the crack of lightning as their lips met, the charge moving through her.

He pulled back, passion replacing the rage in his dark eyes. "I can feel you, you're so real."

"Let's find out how real," she suggested as she reached for the buttons on his shirt. As she parted the wet fabric, she pressed a kiss against his chest— where his heart pounded hard beneath her lips.

Damien shrugged off the shirt, dropping it onto the bottom step. Then, as he followed her up the steps, he pulled his belt free and dropped his jeans on the landing.

Desire slammed through Olivia as he stood before her, wearing only damp knit briefs, which molded to his straining erection. He was so damn impressive, his body all sculpted muscles. She'd never grow tired of just looking at him; he was that beautiful.

But she wanted to touch him, too, while he could still feel her and she him. Taking his injured hand gently in hers, she tugged him quickly up the remaining stairs to the second story. As they crossed the threshold to the room they had once shared, Damien closed the door and leaned back against it.

"Are you really all right?" she asked, concern cooling her passion. A little.

He eased away from the door and shook his head,

his glossy black hair skimming his broad shoulders. "I haven't been all right since you left me—"

"I didn't *leave* you," she assured him, stepping into his arms. Everywhere he touched her, she tingled. Even the air between them sizzled. "I was taken from you."

His hands ran down her back, pressing her tight against him. "I have to find out who did this to you."

"To us," she pointed out.

"Yes, whoever killed you ended my life, too," he admitted, burying his face in her hair.

"No, I mean whoever killed me is obviously trying to kill you now." She touched again the swelling bump on his head. "I think you should get an x-ray."

"I don't want to leave. And I don't want anyone to come here. I don't want you to go away again, Olivia." His arms tightened around her. "I need you here with me."

"I can't stay." She wasn't certain how she'd come to be here, but she was certain she had no future. And knowing he hadn't harmed her, she couldn't take his future away, too.

"Then how am I going to find out how real you are?" He shifted his hips, rubbing his erection against the dip of her navel.

"I'll stay," she said, her voice catching with desire,

"but just for tonight…just to make sure you're not hurt that badly."

He shook his head and ran his fingertips along her jaw. "I hurt," he said. "I've been hurting these past six months. My arms have ached to hold you, my lips to kiss you…."

She had suggested coming upstairs, making love, but now she had no idea what to do and if she dared. "Damien…"

He leaned over and brushed his mouth across hers. The kiss ignited the air between them like the lightning had the fire in the woods.

"You're real," he murmured against her mouth. "You're real to me…."

Only to him. He was the only one who could see her. The only one who could feel her.

Olivia stepped back and lifted her hands to the thin straps of her gown. Hands shaking, she pushed down the straps, and the worn lace slid down her body. Sadness tugged at her, sadness that she'd planned a celebration of their wedding night on the night she'd died. That was why she had worn the gown again. Now they had nothing to celebrate….

Damien's breath shuddered out. "You are so beautiful…."

She lifted her chin and met his gaze. The desire

burning in his dark eyes heated her. "I still can't believe you can see me."

He reached out, his hand shaking slightly as he ran his fingers along her cheek, then her jaw line. "I see you now even more than I saw you before…."

"Before I died?" she asked, shaking her head. "You saw me then." He had been so loving and generous. And after her death, she had suspected it had all been a lie. Now she was starting to believe that his love had been real.

His fingers trailed down her throat to the slope of her shoulders. "If I knew I was going to lose you, I never would have slept. I would have spent all my time just looking at you…."

"Damien, you were very attentive," she assured him. That was partially why she had fallen so hard for him. The main reason had been that she couldn't have *not* fallen for him. She had never felt anything as powerful as her attraction to him.

Guilt and regret filled his eyes. "But I wasn't there that night, when you needed me."

She almost admitted to feeling him in the water with her, but she didn't want to make him feel worse, to have him realize how close he had come to saving her but failed.

"Shhh," she said, pressing her fingers across his

lips. "I have my regrets, too." So many regrets. "But tonight let's not talk about them."

"Let's not talk at all," he suggested as he kissed her fingers.

Olivia tingled. "I can feel you…like I used to. Can you feel me?"

He caught her hand in his, guiding her fingers from his lips, over his chin, down his throat to the smooth, sculpted muscles of his chest. He brushed her fingertip across his nipple, and it hardened from her touch.

"You can really feel me…."

"No talking," he reminded her as he lowered his mouth to hers and proceeded to kiss her so deeply that talking was impossible.

Olivia tangled her fingers in his thick hair, holding on as sensations spiraled through her. She arched, pressing her breasts into his chest. A moan burned in her throat as her nipples rubbed across his hard muscles.

Damien's tongue penetrated the seam of her lips. He teased her, sliding it in and out of her mouth. And his hands moved over her body, smoothing down her bare back, his fingers tracing the curve of her spine, then the curve of her hips. He cupped her buttocks and lifted her. His fingers slid between her legs and slipped inside her—teasing her body like his tongue teased her mouth.

Olivia shuddered and dragged her mouth from his to scream his name as an orgasm rippled through her. She wouldn't have considered it possible, but she felt so alive. With his touch, Damien had brought her to life again.

Then he carried her to bed, and as he lay her across the bedspread, Olivia glanced down. And through her body, she could see the pattern of the satin quilt.

He hadn't brought her back to life, but he made her feel alive. With passion. With desire. He pulled down his briefs, his straining erection freed.

Olivia held out her arms, silently begging for him to join her. To join their bodies. He moved to the bed, bracing his arms beside her shoulders to hold his weight off her.

"You don't have to," she told him, clutching her hands against his back to pull him tight onto her. "You're not going to hurt me…."

But he eased back. "I may not hurt you, but I'll hurt myself," he said.

She gasped, remembering his head wound.

He shook his head. "I'll hurt myself if I rush, if I waste this opportunity to be with you again." He lowered his head, brushing his mouth across hers. "I want to take my time. I want to take all night to love you."

Because tonight might be all they had. He didn't have to say it. Olivia heard the words in her mind and her heart.

"Damien…" She wanted to stop him, to remind him of his injury. But he was moving again, his mouth sliding down her throat. And the way he moved—so quickly and sensually—assured her that he was fine.

He was better than fine. He was perfect.

She clasped his shoulders, her fingers digging into the sinewy muscles, as his mouth slid over her breast, his lips covering every curve before closing over her nipple. His teeth scraped, then tugged.

Energy zipped through Olivia, charging her with desire. "I can't…last…all night…." she murmured between moans.

"You don't have to wait," he assured her, as he slid lower. "You can let go…."

He pushed her legs apart, stroking his hands along her inner thighs before pushing his fingers through her curls. Then he replaced his fingers with his lips—and his tongue, tormenting her.

Olivia clutched his hair, tangling the silky strands around her fingers. "Damien, no…"

He ignored her weak protest and lifted her hips from the bed, his mouth feasting on her. His tongue slid along her cleft then dipped inside.

Olivia's thighs quivered as the pressure built inside her, and as he moved his hands to cup her breasts and his thumbs flicked over her nipples, the pressure burst. But instead of the orgasm stealing her energy, it recharged her so that she had enough strength to wriggle from beneath him and turn him on his back.

And she made love to him as thoroughly as he'd made love to her. First she rained kisses on his chest, then moved her mouth lower over the rippling abs of his washboard stomach. An arrow of black hair directed her from his navel to his pulsing erection.

She cupped her hand around his hot, sleek flesh— sliding her palm up and down the awe-inspiring length of him. And she kissed the glistening tip. Then she took him deeper in her mouth, sliding her tongue around him.

His fingers grasped her hair, clutching her to him—then pulling her away. Her name emanated from his throat in a threatening growl, "Olivia!"

Then he pulled her up, over his sweat-slick skin, and lifted her to thrust inside her.

Olivia straddled his hips, pulling him deep. Holding him tight as she moved up and down. She braced her palms against his chest, where his heart pounded hard and fast. She met his every thrust, passion driving her to relieve the unbearable tension that had built inside her.

Damien arched his neck and pulled her nipple into his mouth. And as he tugged, she came—pleasure crashing through her. Then he filled her, his orgasm spilling from him as he emitted a guttural cry.

He collapsed back onto the mattress with her clutched tight against his chest. "Olivia…"

"I thought you wanted this to last all night," she teased, as she burrowed her face in his shoulder.

Between pants for breath, he assured her, "It will. We'll make love over and over…."

"Will you last?" she asked, worried as she noticed the smear of blood on the pillowcase where his head lay. "You're still bleeding, Damien."

"I'm fine," he murmured, but his eyes drifted closed.

"You're not fine," she said. "You might have a concussion." And instead of making love with him, she should have made him call for real help.

But when she tried to move, he clasped her tighter—his arms strong around her. "I'm fine," he said. "I'm just tired. I haven't slept…really slept…in six months."

Sadness filled her with his grief. "Damien…"

"I can't sleep without you in my arms," he said. "And now that you're here, I can sleep. Just sleep…"

She could have teased him about his claim of making love all night. But she let him drift off for a while. She would wake him in an hour or so and make sure that he was all right.

Olivia didn't need sleep anymore. Or food. Or anything else of this world—only Damien.

Chapter 9

As dawn burned fog off the Lake of Tears, the ghost of the ancient shaman began to fade into transparency like the fog. He was weakening...because of them.

He glanced up at the house, to the bedroom window where two shadows moved behind the curved glass. While his ghost weakened, hers grew stronger. Was she really dead, as dead as he was?

He wondered. And worried.

Centuries ago, he had died, despite his many powers, because of love. The Gray Wolf warrior had betrayed his people and had failed to carry out his *mission to kill the sorceress because he had fallen in love with her. And because of his love for that woman, the warrior—despite a spear through his heart, the shaman's spear through his heart—had managed to hurl the dagger that had killed the Wise One.*

Love had beaten him once. And now, as he gazed up at the house and the entwined shadows, he worried that he would be beaten again. She had derailed his plan—again—last night when she had saved Gray from the icy depths of the Lake of Tears.

So the Wise One needed a new plan. He needed to destroy their love, so her ghost would weaken too much to remain in this world. And so that when she left this world, she would take this Gray Wolf warrior with her.

While her flesh-and-blood heart lay with her body at the bottom of the Lake of Tears, Olivia's emotional heart was intact and aching for the man she loved. Was her restlessness not only over her desire for justice but because she simply could not leave him?

She hovered beside the bed, watching him sleep. Other men's tension and arrogance fell away when they slept, leaving them to look as soft and vulnerable as little boys. But not Damien. He was still intimidating, still tense and ready.

But at least he was alive. For now. Until someone

tried to kill him again. His chest rose and fell with agitated breaths, as if he dreamt horrible dreams....

Or the nightmare that Olivia now lived—in which she only existed. She had no future anymore, but she had to protect Damien, had to make sure he would have one...when she was truly gone.

She studied the sharp lines of his face, framed by the black hair that fell to his shoulders except for the wisp of white across his brow. His cheekbones, brow and jaw looked as though they'd been carved from teak—he was so beautiful. The sheet pooled at his lean waist revealed every sinewy muscle in his arms and chest. She ached to touch him again—with her hands, with her mouth....

His thick black lashes lifted, and he was instantly awake, as if he had not been sleeping at all, as if he had only been afraid to open his eyes and find her gone.

"You're still here," he murmured, his gaze skimming over her naked body like a caress.

"Yes."

"Someone else is here, too," Damien said, sitting up in bed. "I hear a car in the driveway."

Panicking, Olivia grabbed up her gown and pulled it over her head before remembering that no one else could see her. No one but *him.*

He kicked back the sheet and rose from the bed. His

hand going to the back of his head, he grimaced and closed his eyes. A groan slipped out between his lips.

"You should have called the paramedics last night," she said with guilt for having distracted him from the seriousness of his injury.

"You took care of me," he said, his dark eyes flaring with passion as he moved toward her. "All night long you took care of me."

Ignoring her rising desire, Olivia stepped back—out of the reach of his arms and the touch of his seductive hands. "Someone's at the door."

But the knock at the front door was brief, only perfunctory, as the door slammed open against the wall of the foyer. The crash echoed like when lightning had struck the tree and dropped it in a ball of fire in the woods the night before.

"Our guest is impatient," Damien murmured as he crossed to the dresser, pulled open a drawer and grabbed some clothes. He had only managed the briefs and jeans before the bedroom door slammed open with the same force as the front door had.

Anger narrowed his dark eyes. "What the hell—"

"Where is she?" Matt asked, his gaze sweeping the room—right through Olivia.

"Who?" Damien asked. He glanced toward her, his brows arched in surprise.

The sheriff gestured over his shoulder. "I followed a trail of clothes up the stairs."

"Maybe I'm just a slob," Damien quipped.

Color flushed Matt's face as he shook his head. "Not you. You're too careful."

Damien palmed the bump on the back of his head. "Apparently not careful enough."

"No, not careful enough," the sheriff agreed, triumph lighting up his green eyes. "I've got you, Gray."

Damien's brows furrowed with suspicion. "What the hell do you think you've got on me? What's brought you out so early, Sheriff?"

Frustration tightened Matt's jaw. "Apparently I wasn't early enough to catch *her* here."

"Her—who?"

"Your new lover." Matt snorted. "I saw the hole you punched in the wall, too. Yours must be a pretty passionate affair."

Heat flashed through Olivia. And Damien voiced her thoughts. "You have no idea what you're talking about…."

About the extent of the passion that not even death had quenched.

Matt sneered. "Everyone thinks you've gone into seclusion up here at the Lake of Tears to mourn your wife. But I know better."

Damien glanced to Olivia again, his gaze warm. "You don't know anything, Matt."

"I know you killed Olivia," the other man said, his voice shaking with fury.

Damien wearily shook his head. "You're crazy—"

"I can't prove it," the sheriff admitted, rage distorting his face. "But I can prove you killed your first wife."

Damien shoved a hand through his tousled hair and over the back of his head again, grimacing as if in pain. "What the hell are you talking about?"

The triumph brightened Matt's eyes again, and he nearly smiled. "I had her body exhumed."

Damien's eyes narrowed with suspicion, again, and anger. "How come I didn't hear anything about this?"

"I talked to her family," Matt explained. "They gave their permission for the exhumation."

Pain crossed Damien's face again in another grimace—yet this time it might have been more emotional than physical. "But *I* was her husband."

"And her killer."

"It was my fault that Melanie died," Damien admitted, his voice rough with emotion. "But I didn't kill her. She killed herself."

Matt shook his head. "Pretty speech, but it's all lies," he said, dismissing Damien's explanation. "You're good at lying. You even managed to pass the damn polygraph. And you tricked Olivia into marrying you."

And not you? Olivia longed to ask the question. But Matt couldn't hear her, and she didn't want to distract Damien or herself from their discussion.

"That's what all this is about," Damien accused the sheriff. "You have a vendetta against me, because Olivia married me and not you."

"Yeah, I wish she would have married me," Matt admitted, with the honesty she had always respected, "because then she would still be alive."

Damien flinched, as if he agreed with her ex-fiancé. But he focused on her, his dark gaze intense. "I did not kill Olivia."

"Not that I can prove," Matt agreed. "Yet. But I will. But right now I'm placing you under arrest for the murder of Melanie Gray." He unclipped his handcuffs from his belt.

"You've got nothing," Damien insisted, as if he pitied the sheriff, as if he referred to more than the sheriff's case against him.

But what did Damien really have—besides his wealth? A ghost?

"I've got probable cause," Matt claimed. "A full autopsy of your first wife revealed injuries inconsistent with a fall. What killed her was a blow to the

back of the head. She also had other injuries—
bruises on her arms and wrists—and internal injuries
consistent with being shaken—and beaten."

Damien's breath shuddered out. "Oh, God…"

"Are you really that arrogant?" Matt wondered. "So
arrogant that you thought you'd never get caught?"

"But there was a note," Damien murmured. "She
left a *suicide* note."

Matt snorted again. "Read it again. She was
leaving *you*. Guess your ego couldn't handle that, so
you killed her."

"No!"

Matt reached for Damien, jerking his arms behind
his back to slap the cuffs on his wrists. Damien didn't
fight him; shock had drained all the color from his face.

"Is that why you killed Olivia, too?" Matt asked.
"She had finally come to her senses and was
leaving you?"

"No…" Damien shook his head. "She would
never leave me…."

Olivia did not know if he spoke of *her* now or still
of his first wife. Seeing his pain and devastation, she
wanted to reach out—to help him again. But more
than Matt held her back.

Jealousy? Suspicion? She hated how the dark
emotions again gripped her.

"Did you know she was pregnant?" Matt asked.

"Who?" Damien asked.

"Melanie. She was pregnant when you killed her. Did you know that you didn't just kill your wife, you killed your unborn child, too?"

Olivia reeled from Matt's pronouncement. She had known him too long, too well, to believe he would make an arrest without solid evidence. Because he had to have more than suspicion, Olivia's doubts returned—crashing over her.

Could she have just made love with a man who had killed not just his first wife but his second—but *her*—too? And his two unborn children?

Damien stumbled down the steps as Matt, yanking on his arm, dragged him out to his police car—a black SUV with a Grayson Sheriff's Department magnetic badge decal stuck to the door. His pounding head and blurred vision, from a possible concussion, had nothing to do with his current disorientation. He had been able to see *her*—too clearly.

He had seen Olivia's reaction to his arrest. He had seen her doubts, her fear, chase across her beautiful face and fill those pale blue eyes.

Even after last night, after he had bared his heart and

soul to her, she doubted him? She could believe him capable of murder—not just Melanie's but hers, too?

Blinking against the bright sunshine, he peered around, trying to find her. But she had left him again. This time by her choice.

He ducked as the lawman shoved him into the backseat, his arms burning as they twisted behind his back. "So how far along was she?" he asked.

"The coroner said just six or eight weeks." A muscle ticked in the sheriff's jaw as he stared down at Damien. "As if you didn't know…"

"I didn't know."

But he knew the baby could not have been his. Melanie had not let him touch her for months before she died. He had thought it was because she'd been so depressed or that she had grown to resent his lack of attention. Now he suspected she had shied away from intimacy with him out of guilt over her cheating on him.

But with whom? Because that man must have been the one who'd killed her.

His stomach lurched. He doubted his sickness had anything to do with his probable concussion. And bringing up the injury to the sheriff would have been pointless anyway. Haynes would not take him to the emergency room. From the look of hatred burning in the man's eyes, Damien doubted the sheriff even intended to take him to jail. Matt probably had other plans for Damien besides prison.

Like death.

But Damien didn't blame him. If he knew who had killed Olivia—and Melanie—he wouldn't trust the legal system, either. He would have to take care of the killer himself to make sure the son of a bitch suffered for making the woman he loved suffer.

As the sheriff slid into the driver's seat, Damien caught his glance in the rearview mirror. And he wondered if the sheriff didn't take him to jail but somewhere else to kill him, was he doing it for justice or to hide his own guilt?

Because Haynes had been so obsessed with his ex-fiancé, Damien had already suspected the man of Olivia's murder. What about Melanie?

"Did you know my wife, Sheriff?" he asked through the Plexiglas barrier separating the front seat from the back.

Haynes's fingers clenched around the key, which he hesitated before turning it in the ignition. With bitterness and resentment, he answered Damien's question. "You damn well know I did—better than you ever did."

"No, not Olivia." Although he could have argued against the man ever *really* knowing her—Damien suspected he hadn't really known her himself until her death. "Did you know Melanie?"

The sheriff turned fully in the seat, facing Damien through the clear barrier. "God, we're back to this?" he scoffed. "Back to you trying to pass off the blame, trying to pass off your *guilt* onto me?"

"You didn't answer my question," Damien pointed out as dread tightened knots in his stomach. "You have relatives up here, that's how you talked the city council into giving you your job. You must have been up here, visiting your people over the years. You could have met Melanie during one of those visits."

The sheriff shrugged, dismissively. "And what if I did?"

"Then it explains why you had her body exhumed," Damien said, his body tensing with anger and frustration as the metal from the cuffs bit into his wrists. "Because you knew what you'd find."

The sheriff shook his head. "You're reaching, Gray."

"Really? Everyone else believed Melanie committed suicide." Even he had. He should have known better. He should have known her better after all the years she had been there for him, supporting him, loving him.

"You'd be surprised what people really think about you, Gray," he remarked with pity. And satisfaction. "Like me, they believe you're capable of anything."

"Not murder," Damien insisted. "Until you came to town, stirring up doubts, no one had any suspicions about me. They never questioned how Melanie died."

"Because of the suicide note?" Haynes scoffed. "I'll get you a copy from evidence and let you reread it."

If he let him live…

"She was leaving you," the sheriff insisted. "She was saying goodbye to you."

Damien closed his eyes on a wave of regret, remembering the words Melanie had written. *Damien, I'm so sorry. But I'm not happy, and I'm making you unhappy, too. I need to say goodbye. Forever. Staying would only cause us both more pain. You can't love me like I want to be loved. But it's not your fault. I don't deserve your love. I don't deserve you….*

He had found the note after he'd found her body on the rocks. And in the five years since her death, he had blamed himself, believing that *he* hadn't deserved her. Even knowing now that she hadn't killed herself didn't really ease his guilt. Like Olivia, he should have protected her.

"Where's *Olivia's* goodbye note?" the sheriff asked.

"What?"

"The note Olivia left you when she decided to leave you," Haynes clarified.

"There was no note." He'd had nothing of Olivia to hang onto but her ghost. And now even *she* was gone….

Haynes sighed. "That's just like Olivia. She wouldn't leave a note. She was too straightforward. She would have confronted you and told you exactly how she felt."

"In her professional life," Damien agreed, having seen Olivia's intelligence and aggression on the job during the few months before they had married. "But not in her personal life…"

There she had been too concerned about other people's feelings. She had admitted that was why she'd accepted Matt Haynes's marriage proposal; she hadn't wanted to hurt him. But she had when she'd returned his ring.

And she'd hurt Damien when her insecurity and vulnerability caused her to doubt him.

"No, she told you she was leaving you," Haynes insisted, "and you killed her."

"She wasn't leaving me…." Then. But he glanced up at the house, as Haynes backed the car down the driveway, and he caught not so much as a glimpse of his bride. She had truly left him now….

Chapter 10

From the turret window at which Olivia stood, she could not see the police car pull away from the house. She could see only the lake, sunlight glistening on its smooth surface. But she didn't even hear the vehicle's engine, like Damien had. Yet she knew he was gone.

Arrested for murder.

If he were guilty, justice had been served. Finally. And she should return to the lake—and her body—and find the peace that she had been denied with her murder.

But she felt no peace, only guilt—as she remembered the shock on Damien's face. Not just over finding out about Melanie's murder and pregnancy, but also over the way Olivia had looked at him, betraying her doubts.

She had hurt him. She closed her eyes on a wave of pain.

"Oh, God…what have I done?" she murmured, regret filling her.

Behind her the bedroom door opened, and Olivia's hopes lifted. Maybe the sheriff had acknowledged that he had no evidence and had already released Damien. But the person slipping through the door was small and blond.

"Mama?"

Ana Olsson expelled a shaky breath. "He's gone. He's finally gone…."

"Mama?" she called, trying to get the older woman's attention.

But Ana moved to the dresser, opening and closing drawers. "I just don't understand," she murmured, "why he kept all her things…."

Olivia had noticed that, too, when she had searched the house—that Damien had left all her belongings where she had unpacked them on their honeymoon, as if he had expected her back. Or as if he had been unable to part with her things, with even the slightest connection to her.

"He loved her," her mother acknowledged, apparently coming to the same conclusion that Olivia had. "So why did he hurt her?"

"He didn't hurt me." Olivia defended him automatically, with an instinct born of her heart and her knowledge of the man she loved. "He would never have hurt me."

Like she had hurt him.

Ana reached for a picture sitting atop the dresser, a picture Olivia had ignored out of self-preservation when she'd searched the house. The oval, pewter frame held her wedding photo, the one a witness had snapped at the courthouse, of her gazing lovingly into Damien's handsome face—as he gazed down at her, as if she had been his entire world.

"Why did he have to take you from me?" her mother asked, voice cracking, as she returned the picture to the dresser.

"Why did he have to take you away, just like your father had?" Ana asked, addressing the picture version of Olivia instead of the one who stood right next to her. "I lost my baby…again…." Sobs choked the older woman, shaking her fragile body. "My baby…"

"Mama, I'm here," Olivia said, reaching out to brush away her mother's tears.

Ana shivered, as if she felt her daughter's touch.

But she did not turn toward Olivia; she didn't even lift her head as she returned to her search of the dresser drawer.

"Why can't you see me?" Olivia asked. "You're supposed to have a gift."

Her mother had always claimed that their family was special, that one female of every other generation was born with a special ability. Mama had claimed to be that female.

Or was that just your wishful thinking? Olivia wondered, knowing her mother had wanted to be special. *Or am I the one from the generation with the gift? Is coming back from the dead my gift?* But maybe that was just her wishful thinking because she wanted to come back; she didn't want to be dead.

She pressed her palms against her flat stomach. She didn't want her baby to be dead, either, to be gone before the child had had a chance to ever live.

"At least you had me for a while, Mama," Olivia said, trying to offer her mother comfort. "At least you got to hold your child…." Olivia had never been able to hold hers. Her unborn baby lay yet inside her body at the bottom of the Lake of Tears.

Her mother sniffed back her tears and rummaged through Olivia's drawer of scarves and silk blouses. Paper crinkled as she unwrapped something she found in the drawer. A pregnancy test fell into her hand—the pregnancy test Olivia had taken the morning of the day she died.

Pain gripped Olivia, intensifying her loss. She had searched the house, and that drawer, days ago. She would have found the test, had it been there then. But it shouldn't have been there at all; she had brought it with her to the lake that night. She had intended to show it to Damien before—or after—they made love.

Damien had not mentioned seeing it when he had told her about finding her shoes and robe on the shore that night. He had probably been no more aware of her pregnancy than he had been of Melanie's. So had someone put the test in the drawer to frame him? To make him look as though he had killed two pregnant wives? That he was some kind of serial killer?

Was her mother behind the reappearance of the test? Damien had said that he'd first noticed her mother by the house. Had she been inside? Because of her vision, Ana must have blamed Damien for Olivia's murder. But she was wrong, as wrong as Olivia had been to doubt him. To suspect him.

"Mama, don't do this," she whispered as she wondered where her mother had found the test in the first place. Had it been missed down on the shore? Had her mother found it there or somewhere else?

Ana's hand clenched around the test and the paper. And tears flowed silently from her pale-blue eyes.

"Please, Mama," Olivia begged. "Don't put Damien in more danger."

Danger of losing his freedom, the only thing he really had left. The thing she had briefly suspected he might have killed for. But if he had, he wouldn't have imprisoned himself in the house. He would have been gone. But like her, he seemed unable—or un-willing—to leave the Lake of Tears. To leave *her?*

But Damien wasn't just in danger of losing his freedom. Someone had tried, twice, to take his life. "Oh, no…"

Not her mother.

"I know you believe your vision," Olivia said. "But you're wrong about Damien."

Yet her mother would never admit that her vision had been incorrect. And so she might have tried to avenge her daughter's death. She might have poisoned him. She might have struck him over the head.

But was her mother strong enough for her blow to his head to have knocked him out? Relief eased away Olivia's tension. No. Damien was a tall, muscular man. And her mother was small and fragile.

She would have been physically unable to hit him with enough force to render him unconscious.

Ana Olsson might have been responsible for the test showing up the drawer. That would explain her coming back now, after his arrest, to make sure the sheriff had found her planted evidence. But she couldn't have been the one trying to kill him.

"Mama, please *help* him," Olivia implored her mother. "Don't hurt him more. He's been through enough."

Two of his wives had been murdered. Two babies lost before they were ever born. And someone had tried twice to kill him. Why?

Who could hate him that much?

"You must really hate me," Damien said as the sheriff opened the back door of the police cruiser. "You think Olivia left you for me…."

"And then you killed her," the sheriff said, color rushing to his face as he unleashed his rage. "Yeah, I hate you."

"Enough to try to kill me?" Damien asked.

"Try me. Run," the sheriff urged him, stepping away from the vehicle. He touched the holster on his belt and dared Damien. "Run."

"So you can shoot me in the back? Is that your

style, Matt?" Damien goaded him. "Hitting people over the head? You said that's how Melanie died. That's how I almost died last night." He tilted his head, showing where blood matted his hair to the bump on the back of his skull.

"If I tried to kill you, you'd be dead," the sheriff promised.

"I would have been," Damien said with a sigh. "But someone saved me."

"Nathan again?" Matt snorted. "He claims to have saved you from the lake a couple of times. Guilt finally getting to you?"

"Nathan didn't save me last night," Damien said. "Do you know who saved me last night?"

Matt shrugged. "Someone too stupid to know what you are—a killer."

"It was Olivia…."

The sheriff shook his head. "You're not only a killer, you're a *crazed* killer." A ragged sigh slipped through his lips. "Of course any man lucky enough to have Olivia's love then kill her is crazy."

"What about the man who wanted her love but she rejected him?" Damien asked. "Would he kill her out of revenge?"

"You think I killed Olivia?"

"Isn't that what stalkers do?" Damien asked.

"You'd rather have her dead than be with anyone other than you."

Mottled red color flushed the sheriff's face. "I am *not* a stalker."

"Really?" Damien taunted the other man. "So why did you follow her up here, to Grayson? How did you take, hell, how did you *create,* this job?" He gestured toward the back entrance to the sheriff's department, the door that opened onto the holding cells. Off an alley, there was no traffic. No witnesses to whatever the sheriff had planned.

"I took the job here to protect her from *you,*" the sheriff explained. "You don't think I checked you out? You don't think I discovered that your first wife died under suspicious circumstances?"

"I thought she killed herself," Damien reminded him.

"No, that's what you wanted everyone else to believe. That's the lie you told." Haynes shook his head, his anger tempered with pity now. "Hell, maybe you told it so many times that you actually started to believe it yourself. But I'm not the only one who doubts you."

No. Haynes's warnings and her mother's had caused Olivia to doubt him, too. But he'd thought last night would have changed her mind about him, would have earned her trust again. He clenched his jaw so tightly a muscle jumped in his cheek. He had gambled and lost again this time.

Haynes sighed. "And now you want me to believe Olivia's ghost saved you."

"Ghost?" Damien repeated as realization washed over him. "Her body was never found, but yet you're so convinced she's dead. Why? Because *you* killed her?"

Had Matthew Haynes known Melanie, too, and killed her as well? Or had her death given him the idea to kill Olivia and frame Damien for her murder?

"So, Sheriff, what's your plan now?" Damien asked. "To kill me, too?"

"Mama," Olivia pleaded, "you have to hear me. You have to listen. I need your help."

But instead of heading toward the street and wherever she must have parked her vehicle, Ana Olsson headed through the woods, down a path with which she seemed familiar as she ducked under branches and pine boughs without slowing her pace.

"Mama, I need you *now.*"

Damien needed to be saved again—from Matt.

"I know what happened," Olivia said, hurrying after her mother.

Focused on the trail ahead of her, Ana didn't even glance back over her shoulder. Had their connection in life been so tenuous that her mother couldn't feel her now?

"When you warned me that my husband would kill me, I'd been engaged to Matt. I used your warning as an excuse to leave him. I hadn't really believed you," she admitted. "But now I know you told the truth…about *Matt*."

Ana hurried along, so intent on wherever she was headed that she ignored the brambles that caught at her ankles and the sleeves of her gauzy blouse.

"You were right about him, Mama," Olivia said, hating that she had, at one point, actually trusted Matt more than she had Damien. "He killed me, and now he's going to kill Damien…unless you can help me."

She reached out, grabbing at her mother's arm. Ana must have felt her touch, but she shrugged off Olivia's hand as if it were a bramble.

"Mama, where are you going?" Then she recognized the trail as the path to Nathan's cabin. Even if he could hear her, Olivia doubted Nathan would help her. But while he disliked her, he loved his cousin. He would help Damien, wouldn't he?

"Good thinking, Mama," she praised her as they

entered the clearing around the rustic log cabin. A man ducked out of the shadows of the low-hanging front door.

"It's you," Nathan said, startling Olivia into thinking he could see her. But the shaman gestured at her mother. "I've seen you sneaking around the woods and the house. Who are you…to her?"

Ana lifted her chin in a gesture of pride that Olivia knew well—since she often lifted her chin in such a manner herself. "I'm her mother."

"I'm—"

"I know who you are," her mother said, her voice vibrating with fury. "You're the man who killed my daughter!"

"Mama…" Olivia whispered, stunned by her mother's anger and certainty.

While his face paled, Nathan denied her accusation. "You don't know what you're talking about."

And silently Olivia had to agree with him.

Ana stared at the shaman, her pale-blue eyes bright with fear and outrage. "I saw you in my vision."

Confusion distracted Olivia from her urgency to protect Damien. "You saw Nathan, Mama?" she asked.

But the shaman didn't even like her. Even if she hadn't met Damien first, Nathan would have never become her husband. Unless Ana had had another vision, one she hadn't had time to share with Olivia before she died.

His dark eyes guarded, Nathan asked, "You have visions?"

She nodded. "I'm the female from the generation with the special gift."

"Like Anya…" he murmured.

Mama lifted her chin again with pride. "She was a distant relative—a cousin many, many times removed. But she came here and she never came home again." She gestured with her arms wide, encompassing the entire woods. "Because this became her home…."

The woman who had created the Lake of Tears was a relative? That was why Olivia had been so drawn to the lake and the land. And to the man many in town compared to the warrior Anya had loved. Gray Wolf. The ancestor for whom Damien had named his casinos.

"You and your daughter resemble how she was described," Nathan admitted. "Hair like moonlight, eyes like chips of pale-blue sky…"

Olivia shuddered at the description Matt had used for her before. He also had family in Grayson—grandparents and aunts and cousins. Had he been drawn to her because of the legend? Was that why he had suggested they marry on the shore of the Lake of Tears?

"Mama, you're wrong about Nathan," Olivia insisted. "It has to be Matt—"

But Matthew Haynes could not have killed Melanie. Six years ago, he had been finishing a tour with the Marines. What were the odds that both Damien's wives had been murdered but by different killers?

"It was *you,*" Ana said again. "You were the man I saw in the vision. I thought it was him. Olivia was waiting for him, practicing her little speech about telling her husband that she was pregnant."

Sadness tugged at Olivia as she remembered those words. "Husband," she had begun, teasingly, as since their wedding Damien had always referred to her as Wife. "You know why I've been so emotional lately?"

It hadn't been because of unhappiness, like Damien must have thought, that she had been as unhappy as Melanie had. Olivia could not have been happier as his bride except as the mother of his child. "Guess what? I'm pregnant, *Daddy.*"

"She had *this* with her," Ana said, holding up the pregnancy test.

"It was Damien," Nathan said. "He's my cousin, and I love him—but he's done this before…."

Olivia gasped. She had doubted Damien, too, but she hadn't known him nearly as long as Nathan had. But apparently she now knew him better than his cousin did.

Ana shook her head. "It was you. You look like him…only less…less…"

Everything. Olivia had thought the same thing the first time she'd met Damien's cousin—that Nathan was a poor imitation of his much more powerful relative.

Nathan shrugged. "It doesn't matter what you think, lady. No one's going to believe you."

"The sheriff will," Ana insisted. "Especially when I tell him that you planted this pregnancy test. I was in the house a couple of days ago. It wasn't there then. But it is today—the day you must have known Damien would be arrested. I heard you talking to the sheriff."

"You were here?" Nathan asked, his body tense.

She nodded. "I heard you telling him to exhume your cousin's first wife, that you were certain Damien killed her like he had killed Olivia."

"It's the truth, woman," the shaman insisted. "He's my cousin, but he's a killer."

"No!" Olivia shouted.

"No," her mother said, echoing her denial. "You're the killer. And you've been feeding the sheriff lies, feeding his jealousy of Damien, so that you could manipulate him into doing what you wanted. Arresting your cousin…"

Nathan chuckled and repeated, "No one's going to believe you."

"I have no reason to lie," Ana pointed out. "Nothing to gain. I've already lost the only thing I ever wanted—a chance at a relationship with my daughter. Because of you…"

"No…"

"You're the one with everything to gain," Ana said. "The house, the lake, the land… Isn't that what's it's always been about? The power of your *sacred* land?"

"You don't know what you're talking about."

"I know too well," she insisted. "And so will your cousin when I tell him. Damien will believe me."

"Okay then, I take that back," Nathan said with a sigh. "I guess *someone* might believe you…if he ever heard what you have to say."

"Mama, run!" Olivia screamed, shoving her mother aside—just as the shaman sent a dagger flying through the air. The blade struck Olivia, and she screamed again.

Could she die twice?

Chapter 11

"Damien!"

He tensed, fear and panic gripping him, as Olivia's scream echoed throughout the woods. He and the sheriff had come back to see to Nathan after they'd received revealing news.

"Did you hear that?" he asked Matt, who stumbled along the path behind him.

"Hear what?" the sheriff asked, panting for breath as he struggled to keep up.

"She's screaming!" he shouted over his shoulder as he ran toward Nathan's cabin.

Matt called after him, "I don't hear anything…."

"Olivia, I'm coming!" Damien promised as he rushed into the clearing around Nathan's cabin.

"Watch out!" she warned him, her soft voice cracking with fear.

Damien jumped back, knocking down the sheriff as an arrow, the metal tip whining as it sliced through the air, shot into the trees just over their heads.

"What the hell…" Matt murmured, ducking low as they crouched behind some wild shrubbery. Another arrow zipped through the air, low enough that it cut through the bushes and snagged the sheriff's sleeve as he drew his weapon. "Son of a bitch…"

"It just grazed you," Damien assured the other man.

Despite being not much more than a scratch, blood seeped from the sheriff's wound, staining the sleeve of his shirt. "Gray, you are under arrest," Haynes shouted to the shaman. "Put down your weapon."

But another arrow sliced through the bushes, narrowly missing Damien's cheek. He called out to his cousin, "Nathan, you don't want to do this."

"I think he does," Haynes grumbled.

Damien lifted his head and peered toward where Olivia hovered beside her mother, whose crumpled body lay in a patch of Nathan's herbs.

"He's gone," she said, "he ran off into the woods."

Her hand trembling, she gestured toward the direction the shaman must have taken.

"Where'd he go?" Matt asked, his gun withdrawn.

"Woods," Damien said but caught the sheriff's uninjured arm before the lawman could rush off after the man they had just figured out was the real killer.

While they had been hurling accusations at each other, the sheriff had gotten a call with the DNA results he'd requested the FBI lab to rush. Melanie's baby's DNA hadn't matched Damien's—but it had been close, the father also a Gray.

Then the sheriff had admitted that Nathan had been the one to raise his suspicion about Damien. The shaman had offered his guidance to the lawman. He had been the one who had convinced Matt that Melanie had been murdered. He had also been the one who had insisted that Olivia was dead, not just missing.

Only their killer would have known for certain that both women were murdered and how.

But why? Damien had to know.

But first he tugged Matt toward the weeds where Olivia waved him over, her face pinched with worry and fear. "It's Olivia's mother," he said, "she's hurt."

"How the hell did you see her?" Matt murmured

Immortal Bride

as he crouched next to the older woman's body and clasped her wrist between his thumb and forefinger.

"Is she okay?" Damien asked Olivia.

The sheriff answered. "She has a pulse. I can't see any visible injuries."

"She's not hurt," Olivia said as her mother began to come around, her eyes flickering open to stare up at the sheriff. "She fainted...when he threw a dagger at her."

Anger surged through Damien at his cousin and at himself for not seeing how dangerous the man was. He'd considered Nathan eccentric but never insane. Until now.

The shaman had to be stopped before anyone else got hurt. "I'm going after Nathan."

"No!" Olivia's shout echoed Matt's.

"Stay here," the sheriff commanded him. "I'll call for paramedics and state troopers—"

"And he'll be long gone." That much Damien had always known about his cousin, that the man was resourceful. And now he knew how manipulative he was.

"He's got a crossbow. You can't go after him unarmed," Matt pointed out, gesturing toward the scratch oozing blood down his arm.

"So give me a gun," Damien reasoned, impatient to track Nathan before his trail got cold.

"And let you kill him?" Matt asked, shaking his head. "There'll be no vigilante justice on my watch."

Damien should have been relieved that the sheriff did not believe in vigilante justice, or he might have already been dead himself. "So I'll go after him unarmed."

"And get yourself killed," Matt scoffed.

Olivia gasped and beseeched him, "Damien, you can't. Please, don't go after him…."

"He won't hurt me," Damien insisted.

"He already tried to kill you more than once," Olivia reminded him. "Stay here. Please, stay here…."

"Why?" he asked. With her gone, he had nothing to live for anyway.

"Why what?" Matt asked, his brow furrowed with confusion as he gazed up at Damien, completely unaware of Olivia's ethereal presence.

"Why am I standing here," Damien asked, his voice sharp with frustration, "letting him get away?"

Matt glanced down at the woozy woman. "I'll go. You stay with her until the paramedics come."

"You're hurt. You need the paramedics, too," he pointed out.

"It's just a scratch," Matt said, with a trace of their old animosity. "I can go after him myself."

Damien shook his head. "You'll never find him."

"I'm part Indian, too," the sheriff said with pride, reminding him, "my mother was from Grayson."

"I grew up *here* with Nathan," Damien explained. "I know this land as well as he does. I know his hiding places. I'll find him."

And he didn't bother arguing anymore with the sheriff; he just headed off into the woods. Haynes shouted after him, "Gray, come back here!"

Damien ignored the lawman. But *she* refused to be ignored.

"What are you doing?" Olivia asked, following close behind him. Grabbing at his arm, trying to stop him, she warned, "He's going to kill you!"

Damien shook off her weak grasp. "So?"

Her voice breaking with emotion, she said, "I don't want you to die."

"Not even when you believed I killed you?" he asked, pain rushing back as he remembered the look on her face that first night he'd seen her. The hatred. And then the doubts and suspicion as the sheriff had led him off in handcuffs.

"I should have never believed that," she admitted. Regret and apology darkened her light-blue eyes. "I'm sorry—so sorry…."

Damien's heart shifted, warming with her apology…and with the love on her face. For him.

Nathan had been responsible for the doubts planted in her mind. He had manipulated them all. Damien had to put a stop to his cousin's insanity.

He leaned forward and pressed his lips to hers. Like last night, when he had made love with her, his skin tingled and his blood pumped fast and hard through his veins—as if he'd been electrically shocked. Or energized.

"I'm sorry, too," he murmured. For not protecting her. He couldn't make it up to her; it was too late. But he could get justice for her.

As if she read his mind, Olivia shook her head. "Don't do this, Damien. Don't…"

"We'll talk later," he said. "I need to find Nathan." Which wasn't hard; when Damien left the woods he found his cousin standing on the rocky shore of the Lake of Tears. This was where the shaman had murdered the woman Damien loved.

She clutched at him again, trying to pull him back. But either she had weakened, or his rage had made Damien stronger. She couldn't hold on to him. But before he pulled completely away from her, she pressed something cold and hard into his hand and murmured, "Take this…."

Damien glanced down at the antique dagger lying in his palm. "Where'd you—"

"It won't help you," Nathan said, having seen what Damien held. "The weapon is too old and brittle. The blade's dull. It won't protect you."

"Do I need protection?" Damien asked, forcing a smile as he closed the distance between them. "You're my cousin—hell, you're like a brother to me."

Nathan emitted a bitter laugh. "Let's finally be honest with each other, Damien. To you, I'm nothing more than the hired help."

His cousin's bitterness and resentment shocked Damien nearly as much as his being a killer. "That's not true…."

"You don't know what's *truth*," Nathan rebuked him. "You deny your heritage. You ignore the sacred land of our people and the powers it has. You ignore *him*—the ancient shaman."

"I don't want power," Damien explained. "I want *Olivia*. But you took her from me. Why?"

Nathan shook his head with pity and anger. "You don't ask about Melanie."

"You killed her, too. How could you kill Melanie? You were friends." According to the DNA report, they had been more than friends. How had Damien never realized before what had been going on between Nathan and his first wife? Because he had trusted his cousin like a brother.

"I can see the ancient shaman," Nathan claimed.

"The shaman who called himself the Wise One," Damien realized. "The one who killed Gray Wolf? The one Gray Wolf killed to protect Anya?"

Nathan nodded.

"But I thought your guide was his son." Damien recalled the story Nathan had always told him, which was apparently another of his many, many lies. "The son was the real shaman…the one who truly cared about physical and spiritual healing." And not about power.

"The Wise One comes to me in my visions," Nathan explained, "he serves as my guide into the future and tells me what is to come…."

"So *he* told you to kill Melanie?" Damien asked, disgust growing at his cousin's implausible excuse for murder. "And Olivia?"

"He warned of the child you would have," Nathan said, his dark eyes bright with madness, "the child that would be more powerful than even the sorceress who killed him."

"Anya. But she didn't kill the ancient shaman. Gray Wolf did." Damien reminded him of the legend as he edged closer to his cousin.

"Gray Wolf threw the dagger—the very dagger you hold now," Nathan said, "but *she* was the one who caused the death of the Wise One. She was the one who made Gray Wolf fail in his mission and betray his people."

Damien shook his head. "No…"

"She looks just like her," the young shaman mused. "Olivia. She is the bride the Wise One warned of, but I didn't know that then. You were married to Melanie when he told me of his vision. So I thought—" his throat moved as he swallowed hard "—I thought I had to kill her…."

"God, Nathan…"

"Then I saw *her* that day, by the lake. Olivia was the spitting image of the legend, of Anya. She had to be the one." His voice shook with anger and fear. "And then you walked up to her and I *knew*…."

"That's why you refused to marry us," Damien realized, "why you warned me against her—that I'd fallen too quickly and it wasn't real."

"It wasn't real," Nathan insisted. "*She* isn't real. She's only an old legend."

"And that's why you killed her?" Damien asked, even knowing it was hopeless trying to make sense of his cousin's crazy actions, "because she reminded you of Anya?"

Nathan shook his head, his expression one of pity now. "Because she was pregnant."

Damien sucked in a breath at the pain gripping him, as if Nathan had plunged the dagger in his gut and twisted the blade. But, reeling from a sense of betrayal, he turned to Olivia, where she hovered at his side. "You didn't tell me…."

"I was going to," she insisted, tears of regret and loss shimmered in her eyes. "That night…I was going to tell you. But I never got the chance."

Damien sucked in another breath as a metal point pierced his skin, an arrow cutting through the flesh of his shoulder. He glanced away from where blood seeped around the arrow, darkening his shirt, and focused on his cousin.

"The ancient shaman isn't really guiding you," he taunted the other man. "Or you would have struck my heart—like he had impaled Gray Wolf. You would have killed me. Now you're going to wish you had…."

"Damien, wait for Matt!" Olivia shouted.

But Damien could not see beyond the red haze of his rage. He pulled the arrow from his shoulder, his breath hissing through his teeth at the pain of his flesh tearing. "You son of a bitch!"

Nathan was fumbling with the crossbow, trying to get off another shot when Damien tackled him, knocking him from the rocks into the water. His anger fueled strength as superhuman as his fierce warrior ancestor who with a spear through his heart had still managed to save the woman he loved. Damien easily overpowered Nathan, holding him beneath the water.

He wanted the shaman to suffer the fear and panic to which he'd subjected Olivia. And the pain and loss with which he'd forced Damien to live without her.

"Don't do this," Olivia pleaded, as she tread water beside him, her hair and gown floating across the surface. "Please, Damien…"

"I can't let him live…not after he took your life…and mine…." And the life of their unborn child. God, the loss stretched inside him—as bottomless as the Lake of Tears.

"You're not like him," Olivia said. "You're not vengeful. You're not a killer."

"The same blood flows through our veins," Damien reminded her, as he tightened his hold on Nathan, who clawed at his arms, trying to save himself.

Had Olivia done the same thing? A memory flashed through his mind—of Nathan wearing long sleeves despite an unseasonably warm autumn— what most referred to as an Indian summer—six months ago. And he remembered Olivia's recounting of that night, her assurance to him that she'd fought.

She had fought. And not just for her life but for the life of their unborn child.

Nathan thrashed in the water, trying to free himself from his cousin's grip. But despite his wound, Damien didn't weaken. His muscles didn't even strain with the effort to hold the struggling man beneath the water. "So doesn't that make me a killer, too?"

Olivia shook her head. "No, you're a good man, Damien. You are not him. I wouldn't love you like I do if you were…."

"You've had your doubts about me," he reminded her, pain washing over him. "And maybe you were right to doubt me. Maybe I am a killer."

The Wise One stood back, watching the battle between the two young warriors from this modern age of which the ancient shaman knew so little. But perhaps not that much had changed from all the centuries ago when he had truly lived. A woman had caused dissention among these warriors.

She hovered beside the battling men, trying to save the one she loved…from himself. But while her beauty and femininity had seduced the warrior into loving her, she did not understand the heart *of the warrior. She did not understand the warrior was a killer. And that he killed for her.*

The Wise One needed to intervene; he needed to protect the one he had chosen to help him carry out his plan. He needed his disciple to win this battle, to kill off one of the two remaining ancestors of Gray Wolf. Yet his disciple was the other. Would it matter if he died second or first?

Frustration filled the Wise One. The young shaman needed to die second because Damien Gray had proved too strong to die easily. The ancient shaman needed help to put Damien Gray to death.

He needed Nathan Gray. For now. But while he considered how best to assist the young shaman, the woman glanced up.

And for the first time since she had shared his existence, she saw the Wise One. And she uttered a scream of absolute terror.

Chapter 12

The sheriff shut the door of the backseat, locking Nathan Gray inside the police cruiser. "I'll get your statement later," Haynes told Damien.

Damien lifted his arm that the paramedics hadn't bandaged at the shoulder and pushed his hand through his still-damp hair. "I'll be here."

He had nowhere else to go.

Matt leaned back against the magnetic badge on the driver's door of the cruiser and admitted, "I'm glad I finally listened to you."

Damien shrugged and then winced as pain spiraled

from his wound down his arm. Maybe he should have gone to the hospital as the paramedics had insisted. But the bleeding had eventually stopped, so he hadn't needed stitches. And his tetanus shot was up-to-date.

"You had your reasons for being suspicious of me," he allowed, cutting the sheriff a break because Damien had learned that he was capable of more than he had ever considered himself. Like the lawman had suspected, Damien might even have been capable of murder.

If not for Olivia's scream of fear bringing him to his senses, he might have killed Nathan. He had been that out of his mind with rage. Even now he couldn't look at his cousin. And he probably wouldn't be able to face himself in the mirror anytime soon, either.

"Yeah, I had my reasons to be suspicious of you," Matt said with a heavy sigh. "But I'm not sure how many were professional and how many personal."

A grin tugged up Damien's mouth. "I know."

Matt nodded. "I should have listened to you sooner. You saved Olivia's mom's life today. If we hadn't gotten here…"

"But we did…once we stopped suspecting each other…" After they'd learned the DNA results, they had figured out pretty quickly the only other person who could have been responsible for the murders.

"Whatever my reasons, I was wrong about you," Matt said. "I'm sorry."

"If it's any consolation, I was wrong about you, too," Damien admitted. But hell, he wished the sheriff had been the killer; it had been easier to think it was Matt than to know now that it was his cousin.

"It's not much consolation to either of us, is it?" Matt mused as he glanced toward the lake.

Damien followed the sheriff's gaze to where sunshine—but no trace of Olivia—shimmered on the crystal-blue surface. "Nope."

Had he scared her away, with his murderous rage, or was she simply at peace now that her killer had been caught?

"I should have trusted her judgment," Matt said, still focused on the lake. "She was a brilliant woman. And she loved you. She trusted you."

Damien pushed a hand through his damp hair. "She shouldn't have trusted me. I failed her. I didn't keep her safe." Although his heart ached more than his shoulder from his sudden realization, he had to admit it. "She should have married you. She'd still be alive."

Matt shrugged. "We don't know that…not for sure."

Damien turned away from the lake, unable to look at it without her there. "I guess we'll never know now."

"She wouldn't have married me," Matt admitted with a heavy sigh. "She broke up with me before she ever met you. And it was the right thing for her to do. I don't know if I ever really loved her like you loved her, as she deserved to be loved. Or if I only fell for what she represented for me because of the old stories my mother used to tell me about this gorgeous woman from a foreign land, who was as powerful as she was beautiful…."

"She was," Damien said, referring to Olivia, not the long-dead Anya.

"I've wanted to move up here ever since my mother told me those stories," Haynes shared, "when I was a little boy. And every time I visited Grayson, I knew I had to move here. It's home."

"So you're going to stay." Even though Olivia was gone?

"Yeah, I think so." He pulled his gaze from the lake and studied Damien. "What about you?"

"I don't know." If finally having justice for her murder gave Olivia peace enough to leave this world, Damien would have no reason to stay. "Maybe I'll sell the house, the property and the lake and move away."

The sheriff nodded. "That might be smart—to get

out of here. You were talking kind of crazy…about her…about seeing her ghost."

"Not anymore…" He had to accept that she was gone. And it was time he left, too. "I'll stop by the station and give you my statement on my way out of town."

"You are leaving, then?"

Damien nodded. "There's nothing for me here." But painful reminders of all that he had lost.

"Aren't you supposed to be gone now?" Damien asked as he wearily pushed open the door to the master bedroom and found her waiting for him.

Olivia could not read his infamous poker face. So she had to ask, "Do you want me gone?"

A muscle jumping in his tightly clenched jaw, Damien shook his head. "No. But isn't that how it works? When a ghost has justice, they can finally rest in peace?"

"I don't know how this works," she said, fighting to keep her panic from rising again—as it had when she had seen the ghost of the ancient shaman at the lake. "I just know I don't want to leave you."

He closed his eyes then reopened them as if afraid that he would find her already gone.

She glanced down at her body, finding it more

substantial than she'd ever been since her death. "I'm still here," she murmured.

"For now," Damien said, his voice hoarse with emotion, "but we don't have any idea how much longer you'll be able to stay."

She couldn't offer him any assurances, but she could offer him something. "For what it's worth, I couldn't find Melanie's ghost."

"So she's actually resting in peace?" he asked, his dark eyes soft with a trace of wistfulness and hope.

She nodded. "I believe she is."

"What about you?"

"I can't rest yet—not until I do this…." She stepped forward and lifted her arms around his neck, pulling his head down so she could kiss him.

The air between them became charged.

Damien hadn't believed she was really back, that she was really with him, until she touched him. Now he not only saw her—the way he had always seen her, as a beautiful desirable woman; now he felt her—her energy, her soul….

"Olivia, I love you…more than I thought it possible to love. You are *everything* to me." Ignoring the jab of pain in his shoulder, he wrapped his arms tightly around her, unwilling to let her go. Ever. Would his feelings be enough to hold her in this world, with him?

"Damien, I'm so sorry, so sorry for hurting you," she said, her voice breaking with emotion and tears that trailed down her translucent face.

Damien brushed away her tears. "Shhh, it doesn't matter…nothing matters but that we're together."

"For now," she murmured.

"I don't know how long we'll have, but I don't want to waste another minute of our time." He reached for the straps of the gown she wore, the one that had once been so beautiful. He pushed the thin straps down her shoulders, so the lace pooled around her feet. "You're so beautiful."

And so real. The more he looked at her, the more he touched her, the more substantial she became, as if she'd come not just back to him but back to life.

"And you're hurt," she said as she pushed his unbuttoned, torn and blood-and-lake-soaked shirt from his shoulders. Then she pressed a feather-soft kiss against his bandage. "You're always hurt…."

But the physical pain was nothing in comparison to what he'd felt when he had realized she was gone six months ago, lost in the depths of the Lake of Tears. And only her love had assuaged the anguish of that loss.

"You make me feel better," he said, "just being with you, touching you…."

He skimmed his hands from her slender shoulders, over the curve of her delicate collarbone to cup the fullness of her breasts in his palms. "You're so beautiful, Olivia, so perfect…."

Her light-blue eyes shimmered with regrets. "Damien…"

Not wanting to hear her voice any of those regrets or reminders that she wasn't real and their time together could not last, Damien kissed her with all the desperation clawing at him.

Her lips parted on a gasp of surprise at his passion. But then her passion rose to match his. She clutched her fingers in his hair and arched her breasts against his chest.

He groaned as her hard nipples rubbed against his bare skin. And he closed his eyes as sensation, as love for her, overwhelmed him.

She slid her lips from his, her eyes wide with concern over his groan. "Are you all right?"

He shook his head. "No. I'm hurting…."

"Damien—"

"I'm hurting with wanting you," he explained. "I ache for you, Olivia."

She pressed a kiss to his mouth, then his cheek, then his jaw. "Let me ease that ache," she whispered into his ear.

Despite the heat of her in his arms, against him,

his skin tingled, goose bumps rising, as if he were chilled. And he'd actually never been hotter, his blood coursing through his veins like lava.

Her lips trailed along his neck, nipping gently at the skin. He strained to hold himself under control. He had worried that his lack of restraint earlier might have scared her and might have changed her feelings for him. But her love enveloped him with each soft kiss and gentle caress. She tugged at his belt, pulling it from his jeans. Then she unzipped his fly and pushed down his jeans and his briefs.

Damien's erection sprang free toward her heat. She wrapped her hand around him, gliding her palm up and down. Then she dropped to her knees, and her lips replaced her fingers, moving over him in an erotic caress that had him shaking with need.

His fingers clutched in the silky tresses of her pale-blond hair. "Olivia!"

She lifted her mouth from him but kept her lips kissing close to his throbbing penis as she reminded him, "I'm easing your ache."

"Then how come it hurts more?" he asked, arching a brow at her. "How come I ache for more?"

"Because you're greedy," she admonished him, her lips curving into a playful smile that brushed across his pulsing flesh.

"Yes." But he couldn't be greedy now. He had to take what he could get with her and make the most of their time together however long it lasted, however bittersweet it was knowing that their time together was limited.

"Then shut up, Husband, and take what I give you," she advised teasingly, and her mouth closed around him, her tongue flicking over the tip of his penis.

His flesh jumped inside her mouth, his thighs shaking as she sensually tormented him. Her hand stroking the length her mouth couldn't reach, she built the tension in him like one built a fire, stoking the flames higher and higher…until the conflagration burned out of control.

Shouting as he lost control, he came in her mouth. But she didn't release him, her lips continuing to stroke the length of him until she lit the fire again.

He dragged her up off her knees and carried her to the bed. "My turn to torture you, Wife," he threatened.

She shivered with anticipation.

But he took his time. Starting with her toes, he kissed his way up every delectable inch of her body. His lips tingled from the contact with her—with her energy. His hands stroked her, finding all the spots that had her gasping. The back of her knees, the curve of her waist—the inside of her thighs.

She squirmed on the bed even before he parted her thighs. When he stroked his thumb over her most sensitive spot, she screamed and came. So he had to taste, putting his mouth against her, sliding his tongue inside her sweet wetness.

"Damien!"

His body echoing the urgency in her voice, he moved up between her legs and parted her. And he thrust his straining erection inside her. Her muscles wrapped tightly around him, and she arched her hips to pull him deeper. He slid *home*.

For a moment he stilled and savored the sensation—the rightness—of being buried deep inside her. But she moved beneath him, thrusting her hips up and wrapping one of her long legs around his backside.

"Damien," she murmured, pleading for more.

So he gave her more, sliding in and out of her wet heat, setting a rhythm that was too slow for her release or his. He wanted to prolong their pleasure. He wanted to make the most of their time together.

But she clutched his shoulders. In her passion, she forgot about his injury. And so did he. He dipped his head, laving his tongue across one of her dusky-rose nipples as he continued to slide in and out of her.

"Damien!" she cried as she tensed and came, her orgasm pulsing over him.

And he came again—spilling inside her.

She gasped and pulled her hand back from his bandage. "I'm so sorry. I hurt you. You're bleeding again!"

He glanced down at the faint red stain seeping through the otherwise white gauze and shrugged. "I don't care. I don't care about anything but spending every moment with you that I can."

"Damien…" Olivia sighed but lifted her arms to his neck, wrapping them tightly around him to pull his weight down on top of her—their bodies still joined both physically and emotionally.

Maybe more emotionally than physically.

"I want you to stay," he said. And he was the kind of man who had grown used to getting what he wanted. But even he knew there was nothing he could do to make this possible, to bring her back. He wasn't Anya. He hadn't even descended from her but from her stepson.

"I want to stay," she said. "You need me."

He tightened his arms around her. "Yes."

"No, I mean, you need me to protect you," Olivia claimed, her soft hands caressing his back, smoothing over his weary muscles.

"Nathan's in jail," he reminded her. "He can't hurt me." Any more than he already had when he'd taken away his bride and his unborn child. The pain returned, pressing down on his heart, hurting more than if an arrow had impaled it.

She shook her head. "Nathan's not the threat. I saw *him* today, the ghost of the ancient shaman. He was down by the lake."

"Nathan's spirit guide…" His real one, not the one he'd claimed to have. "You really saw him?"

She nodded. "I could tell his ghost was really old, from many centuries ago. But he was really there, his eyes—" she shuddered "—his eyes were so full of hatred."

Was it possible that Nathan's excuse had not been so implausible after all? Maybe his cousin wasn't as crazy as Damien had thought. He'd just been malleable to evil. "So you think it was the Wise One?"

She nodded, her hair brushing across his jaw. "And I think you're still in danger, Damien."

"He's a ghost. He can't hurt me," he assured his bride.

"I could hurt you," she reminded him. "If I hadn't let go of you that first night in the lake…" She gazed up at him, tears wetting her eyes. "I'm so sorry…."

"You've apologized enough," he told her. "And you let me go. That's all that matters."

"*You're* all that matters now," she insisted, "and that you stay safe."

"He can't hurt me," he said again, "because I can't see him. The Wise One is not *real* to me."

"He's real," she said, her eyes wide with fear. "And he emanates evil." She shuddered. "And hatred. The way he looked at you… I believe that he wants you dead."

"We don't always get what we want." Or she would be able to stay with him. Forever. And Damien was too realistic to believe that was possible.

Olivia studied Damien's sleeping face, as she had after the last time they'd made love. Again he was tense, restless—as if unable to fully relax. She reached out to touch him, to stroke his clenched jaw. But her fingers were thin, nearly transparent.

She glanced down, seeing the satin sheets beneath her, but this time she didn't see even an outline of her body. When other people, besides Damien, hadn't been able to see her, she had still been able to see herself…until now. What the hell was happening?

"Damien!" she said his name, her voice cracking with fear.

But he didn't stir, his lids not so much as flickering over his closed eyes.

"Damien!" She reached out, clutching at his arm. But she was too weak to shake him, or to hold on to him. Her fingers lost their grip. "Please, Damien, help me…."

He slept on…as she slipped away.

His face wavered in and out of focus…as if waves of water blinded her. Then she realized she was back in the lake, the current pulling her under, dragging her deep…to where her body lay on the bottom.

"Damien!"

He had been right; now that her murderer had been caught, now that she had justice, she had no reason to stay with him. Except that she loved him, and she didn't want to leave him. But she had no choice—she was dead.

Dead and gone…

Chapter 13

Damien jerked awake as if someone had screamed his name. But he heard nothing, and saw no one. The bed beside him was empty. As if she had never been...

But he hadn't dreamt it—he hadn't dreamt *her*. Although she was gone, he could still taste her on his lips and feel her touch on his body....

She had been with him—in his arms, in his heart. And he had to find her.

He dragged on the clothes he had dropped beside the bed the night before and then descended the staircase in such haste that he skipped every other step.

But as he neared the door, he drew in a deep breath, bracing himself to find her gone. She wasn't in their bed, or the house, and he doubted he would find her down by the lake, either.

She had her justice; she had found peace, which he knew he would never have again—not with her gone.

He turned away from the foyer but the bell pealed, drawing him back. Probably the sheriff had grown impatient waiting at the police station to take his statement. Damien pulled open the door. And his heart slammed against his ribs as he noticed first the light-blond hair. But then the woman turned, and his mother-in-law faced him.

Nervously twisting her hands together, Ana Olsson stammered, "I—I h-hope I'm not disturbing you."

Did she know how much just seeing her reminded him of her daughter, his bride, and that his bride was gone now? Looking as Ana did, she could not help disturbing him.

"No," he said, rubbing his shoulder where the arrow had penetrated the flesh. The bandage had grown hard and scratchy where his blood had dried.

"I thought I'd see you at the hospital last night," she said, her gaze soft with concern on his injury.

"I'm glad you're doing better," he said. "I would have come to the hospital to check on you…" But he had been spending his time with his immortal bride. Except that she wasn't immortal; she was dead.

"I didn't mean that, I thought you'd be there for treatment. You were hurt…." She gestured toward where blood had seeped through and stained the gauze bandage.

He dismissed his injury. "I'm fine."

"I'm glad," she said. "But I don't think you're really fine."

He didn't bother arguing with her. She knew what he was going through; she was grieving, too.

"And I didn't expect you to come to the hospital to see *me*," she said. "I've given you no reason to check on me." Contrition dampened her pale-blue eyes with the shimmer of tears. "I'm sorry."

"I understand why you thought what you had…" Not just because of her vision but because of his cousin's manipulations. Damien shrugged then winced as pain jabbed at his shoulder wound.

"But it was always obvious how much you loved her," she said, her voice gentle. "So I should have known you'd never hurt her. Again—I'm sorry."

Damien could have pointed out that sometimes people hurt the ones they loved, but then that would remind Ana of all the times she'd hurt her daughter, when she hadn't been there while Olivia was growing up. And now she didn't have a chance to make up for not being there for her daughter.

Damien sighed. "I've been getting a lot of apologies lately."

"Yes," she said with a smile. "Matthew Haynes assured me that he cleared you of suspicion."

"I wasn't referring to the sheriff." He had been thinking about Olivia, about how sorry she'd been for having considered him capable of her murder.

"As well as an apology, I also owe you my gratitude," she said. "Matthew said you saved my life, getting there when you did."

He brushed off her gratitude. "The sheriff drove, and he was right there with me."

"He said *you* found me so quickly because you heard me scream." She narrowed her eyes, her gaze steady on Damien's face. "But I remember…I never screamed."

"He must have misunderstood me," Damien said, not seeing any point in sharing that Olivia had come back since she was already gone again.

"Matthew also mentioned that you think you can see Olivia's ghost," she said as she stared up at him with curiosity and hope.

Matthew had a big mouth.

And so she already knew about her daughter's ghostly return. "And then I understood why you asked me if I could see her. *Because you can.* Can you really see her?"

"I *thought* I could," he clarified.

"Now you know better?" she asked, her head tilting with curiosity.

"Now she's gone." Back to the icy depths of the Lake of Tears, he suspected.

"I thought I could feel her, too—a couple of times," her mother admitted, as she lifted her trembling hand to her cheek. "But maybe it was just wishful thinking. It's so hard to let her go."

"Yes," Damien agreed. It was so hard to let Olivia go. *Again.* Losing the connection with her ghost was like losing her twice.

"It's too bad she hadn't been born to the generation with the gift," Ana Olsson said, "then maybe she could really come back to you."

She had come back to him for a little while. And for that time, however short, Damien was grateful; he'd found out the truth. She hadn't left him voluntarily. And even though she'd doubted him, she had never stopped loving him. As he would never stop loving her….

Her mother sighed her disappointment. "But Olivia doesn't have any special abilities."

Damien wanted to argue with her mother, and he

could have listed all of his bride's special abilities: her intelligence, her strength, her beauty…

But his argument would only remind them both of the incredible woman they had lost.

"I brought you this," Ana said, pressing something into his hand.

Damien took the rolled-up paper. When he unwrapped it, a pregnancy test fell into his palm. "This was Olivia's?"

His mother-in-law nodded. "I saw your cousin bring it into the house."

Probably on the day he'd poisoned Damien.

"I didn't know what it was then." Her breath caught with emotion. "But from the way he was acting, I knew it was important."

He stared down at the two pink stripes in the results window. "Positive."

"If you would have had a girl, she would have had a special ability," the almost-grandmother declared with pride.

"I know." That possibility was why two women had been murdered and why two babies had died before their births.

"Of course, that's why the shaman––" her pale throat moved as she swallowed hard "––that was his motive. The sheriff told me what your cousin claimed."

So Nathan had given a full confession. Maybe the sheriff didn't even need Damien's statement.

He nodded. "The thing my cousin must not have realized, was that there hasn't been a girl born in many, many generations of the Gray family."

But yet Nathan wasn't the type to forget anything, not with his having held a grudge over something that had happened centuries before—Gray Wolf, with his dying breath, killing the shaman in order to protect Anya, the woman he'd loved, the woman who had then brought him back from the dead.

"But there have been girls born in *my* family," Ana shared, "for many, many generations."

"You have visions," Damien remembered. "Did you see…?" He couldn't say it, couldn't say "my child" because then the loss would be that much more real, as real as the loss of Olivia.

"My grandchild?" Fresh tears glistened in her light-colored eyes as Ana shook her head. "I only had the vision of my daughter dying. Apparently my gift isn't as powerful as I thought because I misconstrued what I saw."

"I wonder what *he* saw," Damien mused, thinking of his cousin and his spirit guide who had supposedly predicted the future for the modern-day shaman. "I'm going down to the jail. I have to know."

Ana reached out, clutching at his arm. "Won't it hurt more," she asked, "to know what you lost?"

"I already know," he said. "And it can't hurt any more."

But after she left, he glanced down at the rolled-up paper and noticed the handwriting scrawled across it. Olivia's handwriting:

My darling husband,

Meet me by the Lake of Tears for a honeymoon celebration. I love you always.

Olivia

Always? No matter where she was?

Her last written words should have brought him peace. But his misery just stretched like the emptiness yawning inside him. He'd been wrong. It could hurt more.

"Can I trust you back here alone with him?" the sheriff asked as he opened the door to the holding cells in the back of the small police station.

The old brick building only had enough square footage for a reception area and an office in the front, and a few holding cells in the back, where the walls were cement block, the floors cracked concrete and the bars rusted with age.

The building had just been reopened when Matt

had filled the empty position of sheriff. Before his arrival, the state police post in a nearby city had handled crime and punishment for Grayson. For the first time, Damien was glad that Matthew Haynes had come home; it was right that Grayson handle its own law enforcement.

"Yes, you can trust me," he assured the sheriff. His murderous rage had left him at the lake when his fury had frightened Olivia.

But no, it hadn't been his fury. It had been the ghost of the Wise One who had frightened her. She'd been afraid not for her own safety but for Damien's. And she'd wanted to protect him, but yet she was gone.

"Then that makes one of us," Matt admitted with a sigh. "It's a good thing the state troopers are going to take him later today because I don't trust myself."

Damien wasn't the only one suffering. "You really loved her."

Matt shrugged. "It's like Olivia and I grew up together. I grew up loving her. When we met in college, with her looking so much like the woman from the Lake of Tears, from the stories my mother told me, it felt as if I'd found a piece of home. She was really special to me."

Damien nodded. "It was like that between me and

Melanie, we grew up together, too. She was such a part of who I was and who I became. I loved her."

"But not like you loved Olivia."

Damien did not need to answer. Their animosity gone, the two men were surprisingly simpatico.

"I hope someday to love someone the way you loved Olivia," Matt said wistfully.

Damien held in a response, not certain he should wish the man good luck or bad. Loving someone as Damien had loved Olivia and then losing her was hell. But since he liked the guy now, he felt compelled to share his advice. "Don't gamble what you can't afford to lose."

Matt laughed. "You think I'm crazy. But, man, you were happy with Olivia. You may not have had her long, but had you ever been that happy before, as happy as you were with her?"

Damien shook his head. "No. I didn't think it was possible to be *that* happy," he admitted. Nor had he considered it possible to be as miserable as he was now without her.

Something of his misery must have played across his face because the sheriff grimaced.

"Yeah, you're right. I probably am crazy. But I guess it's only fair you think I'm crazy," Matt said with a faint grin, "since I've thought you were."

"When I told you about seeing Olivia's ghost," Damien said, his chest aching over losing her twice.

"Yeah," the sheriff said with a grin, "but I know what caused you to think that now."

"You do?" Had Matt seen her, too? Had she come to tell her friend goodbye?

"Your blood work came back."

"I know. You got the DNA results yesterday," Damien reminded him of the evidence he had shared, which had led them to the real killer. Although now he wondered—was Nathan the real killer or just the *living* killer?

"I got the DNA results yesterday," Matt clarified, "but this morning the toxicology report came back on your blood work."

"So was I poisoned?"

Matt shook his head. "Nothing that would kill you but enough to mess with your head and your health. Your cousin—the shaman—had been slipping you hallucinogens. Not enough to hurt you, but I can understand your seeing things—and people who really weren't there…."

"Hallucinogens?"

"Yeah, some root or something." Matt shrugged. "The lab tech was from Grayson and recognized the unique molecular makeup."

Damien couldn't imagine how the guy had ever studied the molecular makeup of any root or herb from around the Lake of Tears when his grandfather, and his family before him, had never allowed outsiders onto the sacred land. As Olivia had that first day they'd met, the guy must have trespassed.

"It was probably whatever your cousin takes himself," Matt continued, "and claims to see that ancient shaman."

So Nathan had confessed all to the sheriff.

"I was just hallucinating?" Dread pressed heavily on Damien's chest.

So she hadn't been real—*at all?* He could not believe it, not without losing the consolation that her brief ghostly visits had given him.

"Sorry, man," Matt apologized. "I thought you'd be relieved."

On a wave of regret, he closed his eyes. He would rather have been haunted than drugged. Was Olivia only gone because the drugs had finally cleared his system?

"Yeah, you'd think…"

"I'm sorry, man. I know Olivia's a hard woman to let go of," Matt commiserated.

"Too hard."

The sheriff gestured toward the cells behind them. "Are you sure you want to do this?"

Damien nodded. "I have to talk to him. I have to try to understand...." *Everything.*

"Okay then," Haynes acquiesced with a heavy sigh. "I'll leave you alone back here, but he stays inside the cell and you stay out."

Damien nodded his agreement. He didn't want to tempt fate, either, since he didn't have Olivia to stop him from doing something he'd regret—like murder. He waited until the sheriff closed the door on the cement-block room before Damien walked back to the cell in which Nathan lay on a thin, bare cot. No sheets covered the mattress. And the young shaman was barefoot, the sheriff leaving him nothing that he might have used to kill himself.

Shoving a shaking hand through his hair, Damien asked, "So you were drugging me? Slipping me hallucinogens?"

"I didn't want to kill you," Nathan said.

"But I almost died from whatever you gave me," he pointed out.

The shaman shook his head. "It shouldn't have made you that sick. It must have reacted with the alcohol. It was only supposed to make you see things, things that would drive you away from the Lake of Tears."

"You kept urging me to leave," Damien remembered. "For my own good?"

"It was for your own good," Nathan insisted. "It would have been…had you left…."

"And when I didn't leave, you struck me over the head, hoping to drown me as you'd drowned Olivia."

Nathan shook his head. "That wasn't me. It must have been *him*…." And he said again, "I didn't want you dead."

"So you framed me for murder, for the murders of my wives." He couldn't understand his cousin's betrayal of their years of closeness, of what Damien had always considered friendship.

"You would have been safer in jail," Nathan explained. "Safe from the Wise One. You couldn't be allowed to get married again, to have that child of whom the ancient shaman warned me."

"Melanie wasn't pregnant with *my* baby." Damien shared the information he figured Nathan had not had when he had killed Melanie.

Nathan shook his head. "Before he arrested you that day, the sheriff contacted me." Despite choosing to live in the rustic cabin, Nathan had some modern amenities—like a cell phone. "He told me the coroner verified that she had been six or eight weeks along."

"But we hadn't been together for several months," Damien shared. "The baby wasn't mine."

Nathan's brow furrowed with confusion. "But she told me it was—"

"She lied to you."

"No!" Nathan shouted. He sprang up from the bunk and slammed his body against the bars, as if trying to get to Damien. "No!"

"It was *your* baby," Damien told him. "DNA tests proved it—that's how we figured out you were the killer. It's why we came after you yesterday. Melanie lied to you."

"No…" he whispered, his dark eyes wide with horror and doubt.

"I don't think it was just me she was leaving," Damien added. "I think she was leaving you, too. Probably running away from you."

"Why!" Nathan hurled the question as he had hurled himself against the bars.

"No doubt she was scared of you," Damien replied, "and rightfully so…"

Tears dampened his cousin's dark eyes. "But I wouldn't have hurt her."

"You did, though," Damien reminded him. How had he never noticed how truly unstable his cousin was? "You did more than hurt her. You killed her."

"But she was leaving." Nathan's voice broke with pain and resentment. "If she had stayed…"

"I think you still would have hurt her," Damien concluded. "Because you wanted her, and she felt guilty over betraying me with you. I don't think she could have ever been with you and not felt guilt and shame."

"But you didn't deserve her," Nathan cried. "You never appreciated her…the way I appreciated her…."

The truth in his cousin's words brought all Damien's guilt and regret rushing back, but he continued, "Because you knew you couldn't have her, you killed Melanie. Then you 'saw' the shaman later and made up his vision of my having a powerful child in order to excuse what you did to her."

"No…"

Even before learning of the hallucinogens Nathan had been slipping him, Damien had struggled to believe in the supernatural. If he hadn't really seen Olivia, then she hadn't seen the Wise One, and he doubted Nathan had, either. "So then, when I married again, you killed Olivia to justify your killing Melanie…."

"No!" Nathan shouted, his eyes ablaze with conviction and madness. "The Wise One saw your child. He saw the fair-haired girl who would steal away our legacy…."

Damien furrowed his brow, confused by his

cousin's ranting. Nathan seemed so convinced that the Wise One had really come to him that Damien couldn't help but believe, too. And in accepting that, he had hope that Olivia had also come back. "How would she steal our legacy? What legacy?"

"The land," Nathan shouted in outrage, as always disgusted that Damien didn't revere it as he did. "The *sacred* land. And she would be more powerful than anything of the land."

"She would be more powerful than you," Damien said, stating what his cousin was probably too proud to confess. "Isn't that what you were afraid of? Or was that the Wise One's fear? Did he fear my—" he choked back the emotion threatening to strangle him "—*daughter*—like he feared Anya when he ordered Gray Wolf to kill her?"

Nathan's eyes widened with awe. "Your daughter would have been more powerful than Anya."

"How?"

"She would be immortal."

"Would have been," Damien bitterly corrected him, "but you killed her when you killed her mother. My wife. On our honeymoon. You killed my bride, Nathan."

"But it was my mission…."

"But the warrior, Gray Wolf, was strong enough

and smart enough to know when he was being manipulated—"

"The woman, Anya, she manipulated him like Olivia manipulated you."

Damien shook his head in denial. "Olivia never did anything but love me. And neither did Melanie. They didn't deserve to die and neither did the children they carried. My child." He wrapped his hands around the cool metal of the rusty bars and leaned forward as he added, "Your child. You killed your *own* child, Nathan. How's that for betraying our legacy?"

"But the Wise One—"

"Wasn't wise," Damien said. "He was *evil*. He was not a true shaman, like I thought you were. He didn't provide physical and spiritual healing. He provided corruption. And he manipulated you for his own purposes—for power."

Nathan sank to the floor, sobs racking his body as he finally realized what he had done. He hadn't just killed the woman Damien had loved—he had killed the woman he had loved, too. "Oh, God, what have I done? What have I done?"

Damien closed his eyes, unable to witness his cousin's pain without empathizing. But Nathan had brought on the pain himself. He hadn't had to listen to the Wise One. Centuries ago Gray Wolf had, even dead, defeated the powerful shaman.

"You didn't honor our legacy," Damien said. "You killed it off. We're the last of the Grays. You and me. Now there will be no one else. That's what your *spiritual* guide really wanted. He wanted to kill off the last of Gray Wolf's descendants out of revenge."

Nathan peered through the bars at him. "But you can get married again, Damien."

He shook his head, knowing that he would never find the love he'd had for and with Olivia. And there was no point in looking for what he would never find. His life was at the bottom of the Lake of Tears.

Chapter 14

The ancient shaman passed through the bars separating him from the only person who could see him. The only *living* person. For now…

"You failed your mission," he told the young shaman. But what had he expected? After all, the man was a descendent of Gray Wolf, although the old warrior's blood didn't run as thick through Nathan's veins as it did the other man. "You let Damien Gray live."

The young shaman closed his eyes, as if trying to shut out the Wise One's ghostly image, as if he tried to shut out *him*. *He* would not be denied, nor defied. Again.

The man's voice as weak as his will, he murmured, "He is not a threat...."

"But he will have a child," the Wise One reminded his disciple, "and the child will have abilities more powerful than yours—"

"Than *yours*," the young man interrupted him. "That is your fear."

"I know no fear," the ancient shaman insisted, pride filling him. If only this Gray understood pride as clearly as his cousin did. "I know only disappointment—in you. You betrayed me. You failed your mission. If you had any honor, you would do what is right."

"I already told you that I won't kill my cousin," Nathan insisted, springing up from the bunk where he lay. "But *you* tried...."

And failed. But the Wise One refused to admit that again a woman had thwarted his plan when she had pulled Damien Gray from the Lake of Tears after the Wise One had struck him over the head. He would have tried again, but ever since that night his energy had ebbed—his strength fading....

"It was your mission to carry out," the ancient shaman insisted. "And when a warrior fails to carry out his mission, he is obligated to do the right thing."

The young man narrowed his eyes. "What are you talking about?"

The Wise One held out a flower, the soft white petals nearly as translucent as the ghostly hand that held it. "I ask not for you to kill your cousin. I ask for you to atone for your failure and do the honorable thing…."

"You know nothing of honor," the young shaman accused him, his dark eyes burning with hatred and resentment. "You know only power and vengeance."

"Those are the things that make a warrior strong," the Wise One insisted. "Not *love*…"

Disgust filled him, recharging his energy. Perhaps he was strong enough now to attempt his own killing again. He reached out for the young shaman, but the Wise One's hands passed through the bars and through the man.

Nathan Gray laughed at him, at his ineffectuality. "You know nothing of power," he taunted him. "I can't believe that for you I killed two women, two babies…."

"Those were honor killings," the Wise One insisted, "to protect the power of the sacred land and the power of your heritage."

"One of those babies was mine!" the young Gray wailed. "I loved Damien's first wife."

Old resentment and pain overwhelmed the ancient

one as he remembered his long-ago past. "I thought I loved a woman once, a woman who belonged to another man."

"Gray Wolf's first wife?" Nathan guessed.

"His first woman, the mother of his first son," the Wise One admitted.

"And you and the elders arranged that."

He sighed. "I had a woman. I could not claim her as mine. Yet. But I was her destiny. When I told her that, she denied me. She denied her *destiny*…for him."

"So everything you've done, everything you had me do, has been out of jealousy and vengeance," Nathan said, his face twisted in a grimace of pain. "You weren't about the greater good of our people, or of the land. You were all about vengeance."

"They betrayed me!" the Wise One shouted. "Like you have betrayed me by failing your mission!"

"I didn't betray *you,*" Nathan insisted. "I betrayed my cousin."

"Your cousin? The same blood might run thinly through your veins, but you're not the warrior he is," the Wise One goaded him.

"No, I'm not," the young man agreed. "I'm not half the man Damien is. I betrayed him. And I betrayed Melanie and our child she carried. And Olivia—"

"Spawn of the sorceress."

Nathan nodded. "She is a descendent of Anya's. Even before her mother admitted as much, I thought it possible. She looks so much like the legend described Anya."

"That's why the woman had to die. That's why she refused to stay dead. But she's gone now. I have this world all to myself," the Wise One said, satisfaction energizing him.

"So Damien really did see her," Nathan murmured. "I wish I could tell him…."

"You'll never get out of here," the Wise One taunted him. "You are destined to be locked up for the rest of your life. Unless you escape this world, like I escaped it all those centuries ago."

"You haven't escaped anything," Nathan said, shaking his head as if he pitied the ancient shaman. "You're trapped, as trapped as I am…caught between the worlds of the living and the dead. Like Olivia has been trapped."

"She's gone now."

"At peace?" he asked almost hopefully and then sighed. "I doubt it. You have found no peace."

The Wise One held out the special flower and tempted Nathan with a promise. "You will find peace."

His hand shaking, Nathan took the flower from the ancient shaman's transparent fingers. As he passed the petals through his lips, his dark eyes gleamed with triumph. "Now you will know vengeance—*my* vengeance…."

"Your vengeance…?" The Wise One did not understand. Had all the herbs, all the potions, or guilt driven the man beyond madness?

The young shaman dropped to his knees, as the poison weakened him. Coughing and choking, he gazed up at the ghost who had been his spirit guide, his mentor. "When I am gone, so will you…be gone…."

"No!"

This was not how his plan was to have played out. He was supposed to get stronger with the young shaman's death. He was supposed to have some vengeance—some justice—with the killing of one of the last of Gray Wolf's descendents. But the Wise One weakened, as Gray weakened, his energy draining. He glanced down at his body, which faded until it was nearly indistinguishable from the block walls.

"No…"

Nathan Gray dropped to the cement floor, his eyes open in death, staring up at…nothing….

The ancient shaman was gone. He had fed off the young man's energy. And he had only existed because the young man believed in him. But with Nathan Gray dead, the Wise One was finally dead, too.

* * *

"Our baby was a girl," Damien said, his voice carrying on the breeze as he crouched on the boulder. His hand shook as he lifted a white rose and then tossed it across the water. It floated on the surface until the current tugged first the flower and then the stem under.

The same thoughts flitted through his mind as had the first time he'd strewn flowers across her final resting place. *If only I had given her more flowers when she was alive, if only I'd opened up my heart to her completely, as she'd deserved...* Maybe then he wouldn't be forced to live with so many regrets now that she was gone.

"We would have had a baby girl," he told his dead bride, hoping that she could hear him. If he could believe his deranged cousin, they would have had an *immortal* baby girl. That was why the ancient shaman had decided she had to die before she was ever born. Or there would have been no defeating her. She would have been far more powerful than the Wise One could have ever hoped to be.

Damien's head pounded as he struggled with his inner conflict. Could he believe Nathan about the ghost of the ancient warrior? Could he believe anything his cousin had claimed?

Yet if he accepted that Nathan had not only seen but interacted with ghosts, he had hope that Olivia had really come back to him. That he had really seen her again, touched her, loved her…

"You were real," he murmured as he stared into the water, "to me…."

Only his own face reflected back, his eyes rimmed with dark circles of despair. He tried to peer deeper, beneath the water, but he saw nothing. Now.

He shook his head. "You weren't a drug-induced hallucination. You were *real*."

And if her ghost had been real, so had the ghost of the Wise One. Olivia had warned Damien—their last time together—that the Wise One harbored such hatred for him that he was determined to kill him.

"I'm here!" he shouted, raising his fists to the sky. "I'm here. Where are you?"

Birds scattered, rising up from the surrounding trees with a flurry of wings and anxious cries. But Damien saw no ghostly apparition. Only those fleeing birds.

"You want power because you're a coward," Damien taunted the invisible shaman. "You can't face me. You can't take me on. You had to work behind my back, through my cousin, to try to destroy me."

And he had very nearly succeeded. "But I'm still here!" Damien shouted. "I'm still here."

But he had no reason to live, not with his loved ones dead to him. He had no reason but *spite*. A grin slightly lifting his mouth, he settled back onto the boulder, where he leaned across the lake.

"I'm still here," he repeated, some of the pressure easing from his chest, as the birds settled back onto the boughs of the pine trees. "And you're not."

But had Damien once been like the Wise One? Greedy for wealth and power. Was that why he had worked so hard, with his focus so totally on his career, that he had neglected his first wife—sending her into the arms of his cousin?

He had no anger or sense of betrayal for Melanie. He had nothing but regret.

"Power," he snorted with disgust for himself as well as the Wise One. "Power isn't about what you know, or what you can do—it's in how completely you can love." He understood that now…because of Olivia.

He lifted another rose, the white petals as silky as her skin, from the pile beside him and hurled it as far across the water as he could throw. "You, my bride, though you had no 'special' ability, were powerful."

Because she had made him love again despite his reservations, despite his pain. She had made him love her more than he had thought possible for him to love anyone. And his heart ached with missing her…with missing the life they could have had—the two of them and their daughter.

"Come back to me!" he pleaded, casting aside his pride, casting aside everything but his love for his bride. "Come back to me, Olivia. *Wife.* If even only as a ghost, come back to me…."

So he could see her face and feel the electric touch of their connection that even death had been unable to sever between them.

"Olivia!" he screamed her name, sending the birds flying for refuge again, sending ripples undulating across the surface of the lake.

Then the ripples grew as the surface broke, water spraying from flailing arms. A head bobbed above the current. And although water darkened her blond hair, he recognized it—and *her.*

"Olivia!"

But she didn't glance toward him before she disappeared again. He would have doubted he'd seen her, but he caught the image of her body just beneath the water, her hair splayed out like a sunburst.

Damien vaulted from the boulder, jumping into the lake. The icy water enveloped him, penetrating his clothes and burning his skin like fire. The cold water pressed against his lungs, constricting his breath and cramping his muscles, paralyzing his movement.

But he fought against the lake. He fought for her. And he reached her just as the current pulled her deep again. She spiraled down, her arms above her head. Sucking in a deep breath, Damien dove for her and caught her hand. Her fingers were as cold as ice, but he entwined them in his—trying to warm her, trying to hold on to her as the water clutched at her body, pulling her deeper.

Lungs burning for breath, Damien struggled for a stronger hold on her. This time he would not let her slip away from him, not without a fight. He held tight to her hand and circled his other arm beneath her breasts. Then he kicked, fighting against her gown as the strips of lace wound around his legs, threatening to trap him with her beneath the lake. He kicked harder, tearing the fragile material and freeing his legs.

Despite the icy water, adrenalin warmed his body and hope coursed through him with the blood of his Gray Wolf warrior ancestry. Another kick brought him to the surface, and another had them breaking free to the warmth of the spring sunshine that shimmered on the water.

He shifted his grasp on her. Wrapping one arm around her back and his other beneath her legs, he clutched her tight against his chest. Cradling her weight—her *substance*—she felt more real to him now than she ever had since her death. Could she be…?

He glanced down at her face, where her lashes lay like dark fringe against her pale skin—her eyes closed as if in slumber. Or death. She was so pale. So cold. He pulled his gaze from her to focus on the shore, summoning all his strength to speed toward it. His feet hit the rock ledge, and he struggled for purchase on the slippery beach. Her body still locked tight in his arms, he carried her from the water.

Drops of the lake ran down her pale face like tears, soaking into her water-darkened hair. But no breath escaped her lips, which were tinted blue with cold.

"Olivia?"

Was she still a ghost…or dare he believe…

"Damien!" Dirt and pebbles flew as someone scrambled down the rocky slope toward them. "Is it—oh, my God!" Matt Haynes staggered back in shock. "It is…"

"You—you see her, too?" Damien asked, unwilling to release Olivia for fear she would slip away from him again. Could it *really* be her? Not just her spirit but her body, too?

Or was it *only* her body?

"Oh, my God," Matt murmured again, stepping

closer. He uttered aloud the fear to which Damien could give no voice. "Is she—is she dead?"

Damien sank to his knees, the rocks biting through the wet denim and into his cold skin. Cradling her body in one arm, he touched a shaking hand to her pale throat. And his heart slammed against his ribs. "She has a pulse!" he shouted, awed by his discovery, by this miracle. "Get an ambulance! Get an ambulance!"

He did not turn to see if the sheriff followed his order, only catching the scrape of shoes against rocks as the other man rushed away.

Damien could not pull his gaze from Olivia's face as he leaned forward and pressed his lips to hers. She was cold, so cold. He parted her lips and forced puffs of breath into her mouth. Her lungs lifted, accepting his air—accepting the life he breathed back into her.

"Olivia…"

He wrapped her tight in his arms and finally noticed what had only tugged at his subconscious while he had fought the lake to rescue her. The shape of the body he had known so intimately had changed. He ran his hand down her side to the rounded swell of her belly. She had been gone six months—and in that time their baby had grown.

The mound of her belly moved as a small foot kicked against his palm.

Not only was Olivia alive, but so was their baby....

Chapter 15

When Olivia died, her life hadn't flashed before her eyes—but it did now. At lightning speed memories flitted behind her closed lids, and a smile lifted her lips as she recalled her best moments. Meeting Damien, skinny-dipping with him in the Lake of Tears, his proposal on one knee beside the lake, their marriage— staring deeply into each other's eyes as they'd uttered their vows and pledged their eternal love, him carrying her over the threshold on their honeymoon, getting the positive result of the pregnancy test...

Then she whimpered as the memories turned dark,

and pain shot through her head as she relived the
shock and force of the blow, then the immersion in
icy water, and almost killing Damien then saving
him from the very lake that had taken her life, and
saving her mother from the old dagger…then being
torn from Damien's arms, from their bed and sent
back to the icy bottom of the Lake of Tears…

She jerked awake, a scream on her lips.

"Shhh, you're safe," Damien assured her, his hand
tightening around hers. "You're *alive,* Olivia…."

She focused on her husband, on his handsome
face—his dark eyes warm with love. But the beep of
a machine distracted her, and she glanced around the
bed where she lay, with railings on the sides. Tubes,
one in her nose, one in her arm, and machines, some
of them beeping, some flashing numbers, were
hooked to her. "I'm in a hospital?"

"But you're going to be fine," he said, leaning
forward to kiss her fingers, which he then entwined
with his. "You came back to me."

She shook her head, confused. "But I'm dead,
Damien. I'm dead."

A smile curved his lips. "No, you're not."

Had it all been a dream?

Or was *this?* She reached out, trying to touch his
face, but as she leaned forward, she noticed some-

thing else. Her belly had swelled to a huge mound. She pressed a hand against her side, where a small foot kicked. "I'm dreaming…."

She had to be dreaming.

Or maybe this was heaven. With her baby still in her womb and Damien at her side, she was finally at peace. And so she slipped back into sleep.

With a shaking hand, Damien pulled shut the door of the hospital room, squeezing one last glance through the crack. At Olivia. She lay quietly in the bed, as quietly as she'd lain in his arms when he had pulled her from the water. But she wasn't dead. Now. Or then.

"I'll get you if she wakes up again," her mother assured him before the door closed. Like Damien, she was unwilling to leave her daughter's bedside. Ana Olsson probably shared his fear that if they did, they would lose Olivia again.

"I can't believe it," the sheriff murmured, from where he leaned wearily against the wall of the corridor. "It's not possible…."

"You have roots here, people here," Damien said, "you've heard all the legends. So you should know that *anything* is possible on this special land." Especially with this special woman.

Matt gave a jerky nod. "I should know, given what happened at the jail…."

Damien closed his eyes on a wave of regret and acceptance. And even though he was pretty certain he already knew, he asked, "What happened?"

"Your cousin is dead. He killed himself— somehow." The sheriff shuddered. "It was weird— the lights dimmed in the whole station as if something was pulling on the circuits, almost as if he was being electrocuted. But he must have eaten something, some kind of flower or plant that was poisonous. I'm having the coroner run a toxicology screen. But I don't know where he got whatever he took. I thoroughly searched him when I arrested him."

"You did," Damien assured him, trying to allay the man's obvious sense of guilt. He could tell the lawman where he thought the flower had come from, but he doubted Matt wanted to hear any more about ghosts.

"It was so strange—all the lights dimming the way they did. And I think I heard something— someone yelling 'no.' But it didn't sound anything like a human voice." Matt shuddered again. "Creepiest thing I ever heard…"

It hadn't been a human voice, at least not a living

human. Nathan had not just taken his own life; he had taken the life of the ancient shaman who had tried to live through him. At the lake, before Olivia had surfaced, Damien had had that odd feeling as his tension had eased. And he'd known the ancient shaman was gone.

"But it had to be your cousin's voice," Matt assured himself even though fear lingered in his eyes. "I'm sorry he's gone…."

Damien wasn't so sure Nathan was really gone. He would probably come back, like Olivia had, like the Wise One had. But knowing how much his cousin regretted his actions, Damien believed Nathan would return as the shaman he should have been, the one to aid physical and emotional healing.

Maybe, to make amends for what he'd done, Nathan had helped free Olivia from the bottom of the Lake of Tears. Maybe he had helped her return to Damien.

Matt sighed. "Anyway, that's why I came to the house this afternoon, to tell you about Nathan's death. But when you weren't inside, I thought—"

"You thought I was killing myself, too," Damien surmised.

"It occurred to me that you might try to join her in the lake," Matt admitted. "So I went around the house to check on you."

Damien's mouth curved into a slight grin. "And found me in the water."

"For a minute I thought I was right, that you were drowning yourself," Matt admitted. "Then I saw that you were actually coming out of the lake with *her* in your arms."

Damien's grin widened with a happiness he had thought he would never again experience.

Matt's brow furrowed with confusion. "How is that possible? She couldn't have been in the water for six months—and survived."

Damien shrugged.

"So Nathan hadn't killed her," the sheriff said, floundering for the logical explanation. "He must have been holding her somewhere, keeping her hostage."

"Nathan confessed to killing her," Damien reminded the lawman.

"But she's alive."

"Now."

Matt shook his head, obviously still struggling to believe that the impossible was possible even in Grayson. "Will Olivia be okay?"

Damien's heart swelled with warmth and happiness. "The doctors believe she will make a full recovery and come back to us completely."

"That's great." Matt nodded and conspicuously refrained from asking about the baby. He probably doubted that, as malnourished as Olivia had appeared, that the baby would survive.

But Damien had faith now.

"It's a miracle," he said.

And miracles were not only possible, they were probable.

Olivia's perfect dream hadn't lasted, something she discovered as she awoke later and reached for her stomach. "Noooo!"

The mound, and the little kicking foot, was gone—her stomach nearly flat and empty beneath a silk-and-lace gown that tied at her shoulders.

She lifted her head, gazing around the paisley-papered bedroom in the second story of the turret. Like her, it was empty. "Damien? Damien!"

Where was he? Had he left her, too?

"The baby," she screamed, her voice and heart breaking as she relived her loss. "The baby's gone!"

Had Olivia only dreamt her pregnancy? Had she dreamt it all?

"Help me!" she shouted.

Frantic, she summoned the energy to swing her legs over the side of the bed. As her feet hit the plush rug, she wobbled—and dizziness lightened her head.

She had to find them—Damien and the baby. Drawing in a deep breath, she gathered her strength and headed toward the closed door. Pain stung her arm as IV tubing pulled at her skin. She yanked the tubes free and continued, staggering, toward the door, which drew open as she neared it.

"Olivia! Oh, thank God you're awake!" Damien exclaimed, then he reached for her, swinging her up in his arms. "But what are you doing out of bed?"

Her breath shuddered out in a ragged sob, and she clung to him, pressing her head against his chest. His heart beat hard beneath her cheek.

"You're real," she murmured, tightening her arms around him, unwilling to ever let him go again.

"I have to keep checking to make sure you're real," he admitted. Then he lowered his head and pressed his lips against hers.

Just as when she had been a ghost, electricity charged between them, and she felt more than his kiss, more than his touch—she felt his soul.

As he lay her back onto the bed, their mouths parted. But he leaned forward, settling beside her, and kissed her again, pressing his lips to her forehead. "You're so beautiful. And so alive…"

Olivia pressed a palm against her nearly flat stomach. And so empty…

"Damien?" Tears stung her eyes, but she blinked them back. "What about—" her breath caught, burning in her throat "—what about…our baby?"

His hand covered hers and squeezed. "She's beautiful, too, just like her mama."

Hope warmed her like the sunshine pouring through the curved windows warmed the room. And the tears, of relief and happiness, flowed now. "She's alive?"

"Oh, honey, I thought you knew." He cupped her face, brushing away her tears with his thumbs.

"Knew what?" she asked, confusion muddling her mind. "I feel like I don't know anything anymore. I don't know what's real and what's not. Tell me everything, please!"

His dark eyes shining, he grinned. "I will. I'll tell you *everything*. I just don't know what you already know and what you don't know. And what you'll believe…"

She closed her eyes as images flashed through her mind again—like they had when she'd awakened in the hospital. She remembered that and more. So much more…

But none of that mattered now. She asked about what was closest to her heart. "You said *she?*" Her voice cracked as emotion choked her. "We have a *daughter?*"

Beaming with a father's overwhelming pride, he replied, "Yes, we do. We have a beautiful, amazing baby girl. She's a miracle."

"But—but how?" She remembered dying, drowning in the Lake of Tears. She lifted her hands, holding them in front of her face, checking to see if she was real.

"You went into labor," Damien answered her literally, misunderstanding her confusion. "But you were still so weak that they had to take her caesarian."

"But wouldn't it be too soon?" Olivia asked, trying to remember how much time had passed when she'd been dead.

"The doctors estimated that she was about twenty-nine weeks," Damien said.

"Then she would be too small, especially with my having no prenatal care. All those months I spent at the bottom of the lake, she would have had no nourishment." Olivia pressed a hand against her stomach. "And I don't feel like I had surgery at all."

Was Damien lying to her about the baby, trying to make her feel better about having not protected their child?

"There's no way I could have had her," Olivia said, her heart aching again over the loss of her child. But she remembered her swollen belly when she had awakened in the hospital.

"You had our baby," Damien assured her. "And you're healed now."

"But it would take weeks for the incision to heal." Realization dawned. "It's been weeks, hasn't it?"

His fingertips skimmed along her jaw, as if he were unable—or unwilling—to stop touching her. "Ever since you came back from the lake, *really* came back," he said, "you've been in and out of it, getting your strength back, even before you went into labor."

But Olivia didn't care about herself. "Tell me about her. Is she really all right?"

"I'll do more than tell you," he said, rising from the bed. "I'll show you our baby girl."

Eager to see their miracle child, strength infused Olivia and she sat up on the side of the bed. "I'll get dressed and go with you."

Cupping her shoulders, Damien guided her back down to the bed. "Rest. I'll bring her to you."

Olivia stared up at him. "Bring her to me? How?"

"She's just down the hall," Damien explained with a smile, "in the nursery."

Olivia didn't remember the Victorian house as having had a nursery. When she had discovered she was pregnant, that was something she had intended to talk to Damien about—about making the house on the lake their home and redecorating a room specifically for their baby. But she had been denied that chance. "Nursery?"

Color flushed Damien's naturally tanned skin. "We have a nursery now. For her. I hope you like it. I had no idea what I was doing, but your mother helped."

"My mother?"

"Ana has been staying with us," he explained, his voice warm with affection and gratitude, "helping me take care of you and our daughter."

"Our daughter?" Tears stung her eyes as emotion overwhelmed her. "She's home? She's really home?"

Damien, his hands around her arms, lifted her from the bed and lowered his head. His mouth brushed over hers in a gentle kiss. "You're both home."

Olivia shook her head, unable to understand or believe what had happened. "I don't understand how is any of this is possible...."

Chapter 16

Love filled Damien's heart as he leaned against the doorjamb and studied his wife and daughter. Olivia sat in the rocker, the baby cradled in her arms. But she didn't move, as if she dared not over fear that moving might shatter the moment. She stared down at the baby girl, her eyes wide with awe and doubt.

"She's real," he assured her, even though he had struggled to accept that himself.

They were so beautiful—mother and daughter. The baby had his dark hair but Olivia's pale skin and blue eyes.

"How?" Olivia asked. "I was in the lake for months. I was dead."

"But *she* wasn't dead," he pointed out.

She glanced to him, her brow furrowed. "You think she brought me back to life?"

"I'm sure of it."

"You think that's her gift," Olivia asked, "that she can bring back the dead?"

"She has a special gift like your mother. She is a descendent—*you* are a descendent—of Anya's," Damien explained.

"The woman who created the Lake of Tears?" She nodded. "I heard my mother tell Nathan that Anya was a cousin many, many times removed."

"She fell for a warrior—my great, great, great, great grandfather. He was supposed to kill her, but they fell in love." Even though Olivia knew the story, Damien felt compelled to retell it—to point out the parallels to their lives, their love.

"And even though he was pierced through the heart with a spear, he saved her from his people." She recalled the legend and gazed up at Damien, her eyes soft with love.

"He saved her from the shaman who wanted her dead by throwing a dagger in his heart."

Olivia's mouth curved into a smile at their tag-team retelling of the story. "But the warrior was already dead and fell in the ravine."

"And her tears filled the ravine, bringing him back to her, as you came back to me," Damien said, his heart swelling with love for his bride.

"And she brought him back to life. That was Anya's gift—being able to resurrect the dead." She turned her attention to their daughter. "So that's your gift, too, little girl," Olivia mused, playing with the baby's tiny, grasping hand. "She brought me back to life."

"I believe she did," Damien said, and then he shared what his cousin had about the ancient shaman's vision. "And the reason she was alive to do it, even when you were dead, is because *she* can't die."

Olivia lifted her gaze to him, her eyes narrowed in confusion. "What do you mean?"

"She was born too early," he admitted, "and malnourished, but she didn't even need critical care. She survived."

Olivia stared down at their daughter and touched a trembling hand to her soft black hair. "She's immortal."

"The ghost of the ancient shaman warned Nathan that she would be," Damien shared. "That I would have a daughter who could not die."

"And because he wanted no one to have more

power than he had, the shaman ordered Nathan to kill her before she was born," Olivia deduced, her intelligence matching her beauty.

"But he was too late."

"He hates you," Olivia said, fear stealing the happiness from her face. "Even though he can't hurt our child, he'll try to hurt *you* again."

"He's gone," Damien assured her.

"But you can't know that for sure," she said, worried. "You never saw him."

"Nathan's dead."

She gasped.

"I didn't—I had nothing to do with it," he assured her, with a pang of regret that she could still doubt him. "He killed himself. And by taking himself out of this world, he took out the Wise One, too. Without Nathan to believe in him and hold him in this world, the ancient shaman ceased to exist."

She expelled a shaky sigh of relief. "I know that you didn't kill Nathan."

"I had nothing to do with it," he repeated. He had never manipulated his cousin as the shaman ghost had.

"But he killed himself because of you," Olivia said, her voice soft and gentle, "because of what he'd done to you. Despite everything he did, I really believe your cousin loved you."

Damien's lips curved in a bittersweet smile. "I think so, too. And I like to believe he helped bring you back to me from the bottom of the Lake of Tears."

Cradling their child in her arms, Olivia stood and carried the baby to the bassinet, and settled the child inside the white wicker basket. "And I would rather believe it was her," she said as she gazed down with awe on the sleeping baby, "our daugh-.ter, who brought me—who brought *us*—back to you."

"I was sitting on the boulder when you surfaced," Damien said.

She lifted her gaze to his. "The boulder from where Anya had wept the tears that filled the ravine?"

He nodded.

"The one with my memorial plate on it."

"That's been taken off now," he assured her. "But I was sitting there, begging for you to come back to me, and you came back to me."

Olivia smiled. "You begged?"

"Only for you," Damien said, knowing she mocked his stubborn pride. "And it worked—you came back to me."

"Your love brought me back," she said.

"I think so," he agreed. "Love is more powerful than any special ability."

She turned back to the bassinet, stared down at their daughter and emitted a wistful sigh. "Yes, it is."

"You're tired," Damien said, rushing to her side. "You should get back to bed."

"No, I'm not tired," she insisted. "I'm relieved. Do you realize that we never have to worry about our daughter the way other parents worry?"

Damien stared over her shoulder at their tiny child. "Oh, we'll still worry. Her body might be invincible, but her heart can still get broken. Her feelings can still get hurt."

Olivia bit her bottom lip. "You're right. We'll still worry."

"I'm worried about *you* now."

"So carry me back to bed," she said.

Damien lifted her, holding her body close to his heart, and turned toward the door.

"Wait," she said, "I want to look at her one more time. She's so beautiful, so perfect. And so is this room. It's a perfect nursery, Daddy." She gestured around at the sunshine-yellow paint and the animal stencils. "Thank you for making this special for her and for making this our home. I know you never wanted to live here."

"I do now," he said. "It is our home and will always be her home."

"Damien…"

"But I also want to open up the property to the public," he admitted, wondering how she would feel about his decision.

"For weddings?"

He shook his head. "For research. I want to see if any of the plants and flowers that grow *only* here can help people, can cure diseases."

Tears shimmered in her eyes as she stared up at him. "You can't be real," she said.

"Why?"

"Because you're too good to be true."

He grinned.

"It's a wonderful idea."

His grin faded. "And long overdue. I should have thought of it years ago." But he had been too busy thinking about other things, things that hadn't mattered. Like wealth. And possessions. Now he knew that all that really mattered was love. "And your getting back to bed is long overdue, Wife."

As he carried Olivia through the doorway, her mother appeared, her eyes glistening with emotion.

"I heard you on the baby monitor," Ana admitted, indicating the white plastic receiver in her hand. "But I didn't want to intrude. I'm sorry, though, I couldn't wait any longer. Olivia, my darling, are you all right?"

"I'm fine, Mama," Olivia assured the older woman. "Thank you for being here for me."

Tears spilled out of Ana's eyes. "I'm so sorry I wasn't there for you when you were growing up, or whenever you needed me. I'm so sorry…."

Olivia shook her head. "You're here now, Mama. And you've been here for me, for my *family,* when it really mattered most."

"I'd like to stay," Ana said with a quick glance up at Damien.

He had already asked her with the stipulation that Olivia, when she awoke, had the final say.

Olivia glanced up at him, too, with a question in her eyes. A question he answered with a nod. "I'd love for you to stay with us, Mama. Then our family will be complete."

And mother and daughter would have the time they both needed to reconnect.

"Our family," Ana murmured and mouthed a thank-you at Damien. Then she turned her attention toward the bassinet.

"The baby's sleeping," Olivia assured her.

"The baby…" Damien murmured. "She needs a name."

"You haven't given her a name?" Olivia asked, turning to him in surprise.

Damien shook his head. "Not without you."

Her brow furrowed in confusion. "But you know what we have to name her."

"Of course," he said with a grin. "Anya."

"Anya Gray," the baby's grandmother said with a nod of approval. She reached out, brushing Olivia's hair back from her face. "Now, you get some rest. I'll watch over your beautiful daughter."

Damien suspected she wasn't the only one watching over this Anya. Since accepting that anything was possible, he had become attuned to the land…and the spirits that hadn't quite been able to leave it. The ancient shaman was gone, but generations of Grays remained, offering him protection and guidance and love.

Damien shouldered open the door to their bedroom, which Olivia swung closed behind them. "You're right, Wife. There was no other name for her."

As he laid her on the bed, Olivia hooked her arms around his neck and pulled him down with her.

"I thought you were tired," he said with a chuckle of surprise. "You wanted me to carry you…."

"Just to save my strength," she explained, "for this." She tunneled her fingers into his hair and pulled down his head for her kiss.

Damien lost himself in the softness of her lips

and the warmth of her mouth. He had waited so long for this and had wanted her for so long. But, breathing hard, he pulled back and shook his head. "We can't do this…."

Olivia arched her hips and rubbed against the erection straining the fly of his jeans. "Oh, I think you can…."

He chuckled at her challenge. "I can, but you're not strong enough yet."

"I've spent enough time living in limbo, Damien. I want to really live. I want to love *you*. Completely."

His hand shaking slightly, he cupped her cheek in his palm. Her skin was like silk against his. "Are you real?"

"I'm real," she promised. "Let me show you how real I am." She lifted her hands to the straps tied loosely at her shoulders and tugged the knots free. The gown, silk and lace, like her bridal negligee, slipped down her body, baring her breasts for his hungry gaze.

And touch. He skimmed his hand from her face, down her throat to where her heart beat hard and fast beneath his palm. "You're alive."

"I'm alive," she repeated, as in awe of the miracle as he was. "And I'm so in love with you."

She moved her fingers to his shirt, clutching the

fabric and tugging it up over his stomach. Her knuckles brushed his abdomen, and they both sucked in a breath in reaction.

He pulled the shirt over his head and tossed it on the floor. Then he stood up and unzipped and kicked off his jeans and briefs.

Olivia moaned, her nipples peaking at the just the sight of his nakedness. Pride filled him that he could affect this woman as deeply as she affected him. Wanting her as naked as he was, he pulled the gown, which had pooled at her waist, from her body. Then, hooking his finger in the elastic, he tugged off the last scrap of lace that would separate skin from skin, and he settled onto the bed next to her. The mattress dipped, and she rolled to her side and pressed tight against him.

Her breast rubbed against his chest, where his heart pounded for her—fast and hard, like the beat of a war drum.

"I am so in love with you," he said, his breath catching at the emotions surging through him. He lowered his head, touching his lips to hers—gently, not wanting to overwhelm her with the passion he could barely control.

But her tongue slid inside his mouth, teasing his with playful forays. And she lifted her leg, sliding the silky skin of her inner thigh against his hip.

His erection pulsed, pressing against her navel, straining for release. He swallowed a groan and tangled his fingers in her hair, holding her head as he deepened the kiss.

She arched, pressing the soft fullness of her breasts against his chest and rubbing until their skin created a delicious friction. And like an electrical charge, the air sparked between them, alive with their passion.

He dragged his mouth from hers, panting for breath. "Olivia…"

Her hands slid over his body, caressing the tensed muscles of his neck and back, gliding lower to grasp his buttocks and urge him closer. She was driving him out of his mind. Again.

"Do you want me to beg again?" he asked.

She shook her head. "You don't have to beg," she assured him. "I'm here. Take me. Before I beg for you. I need your touch, Damien. I need to know this is real and not just a perfect dream. I need to feel."

"You don't feel this?" he asked, sliding his hand over the curve of her hip to stroke the thigh she rubbed against him. He leaned forward, nuzzling her neck with his mouth and pressing kisses to her sweet skin.

She shivered. "It's not enough. I want more…."

So he rolled her, pressing her onto her back. And he moved down her beautiful body, covering every silky inch with his mouth. Leaving a trail of kisses from her collarbone, over the curve of her breast to the dusky-rose nipples that begged for his touch.

As he closed his lips around one nipple and tugged, she moaned and shifted on the sheets. And he knew the pressure building inside him built in her, too, demanding release. He could deny her nothing. He skimmed his knuckles along her stomach, across the healed scar where the doctors had taken their child, and then he slid his fingers through her curls until he found her wet heat.

She arched her hips as he eased a finger inside her and swirled it. Her light blue eyes widened with pleasure. "Damien!"

He continued to suckle at her breast, teasing the nipple to a hard point, as he slid another finger inside her and intimately stroked her.

She writhed. "Damien, please, it's not enough…."

"You want more?"

She reached between them and wrapped her fingers around his penis. Then she glided her hand up and down his shaft. "I want you—all of you."

"You have me," he assured her. "All of me." He couldn't hold anything of himself back from her again. She owned him heart and soul.

She lifted her legs, wrapping them around his

waist, and Damien drove home, thrusting his pulsing penis inside her. She gasped at his invasion, her inner muscles clutching at him. Then she moved, arching her hips, meeting his thrusts. She held tight to his shoulders, her nails biting his skin. Her pale skin flushed and her eyes glazed with passion, Olivia stared up at him.

He lowered his head, kissing her, making love to her mouth as he made love to her body. And he reached between them, stroking first her breasts then lower, near where their bodies joined.

Heat scorched him as she came, her orgasm pouring over him. And knowing that she was strong enough to handle him, he pounded into her with deep thrusts until his body tensed—then the tension exploded. And he came, shouting her name.

Olivia wrapped her arms around his back, holding him tight, pulling his weight down on top of her.

"I'm going to crush you," he warned, between pants for breath.

She shook her head, tangling her hair around their faces. "No. I'm invincible," she said.

"You're my immortal bride," he agreed, his heart overflowing with love for her and their child. "Because of our daughter."

"Because of *your* love."

"*Our* love," he corrected her, rolling to his side but holding her tight in his arms.

With a wistful sigh, Olivia nuzzled into his neck, pressing a kiss against his pounding pulse. "Our *immortal* love."

She was right. No matter how long either of them lived, their love would never die. He pressed a kiss against her forehead and closed his eyes, finally able to succumb to sleep and trust that she would still be there, with him, when he awoke again.

"Yes," he agreed, "our immortal love."

* * * * *

The story of Gray Wolf and Anya—
RESURRECTION
by Lisa Childs—is available in e-book form from
Silhouette Nocturne Bites. Go to eHarlequin.com,
or your e-book retailer, and enjoy it today!

*Celebrate 60 years of pure reading pleasure
with Harlequin®!
Silhouette® Romantic Suspense is celebrating with
the glamour-filled, adrenaline-charged series
LOVE IN 60 SECONDS starting in April 2009.*

*Six stories that promise to bring the glitz of
Las Vegas, the danger of revenge, the mystery of a
missing diamond, family scandals and ripped-
from-the-headlines intrigue. Get your heart racing
as love happens in sixty seconds!*

*Enjoy a sneak peek of
USA TODAY bestselling author
Marie Ferrarella's
THE HEIRESS'S 2-WEEK AFFAIR
Available April 2009
from Silhouette® Romantic Suspense.*

Eight years ago Matt Shaffer had vanished out of Natalie Rothchild's life, leaving behind a one-line note tucked under a pillow that had grown cold: *I'm sorry, but this just isn't going to work.*

That was it. No explanation, no real indication of remorse. The note had been as clinical and compassionless as an eviction notice, which, in effect, it had been, Natalie thought as she navigated through the morning traffic. Matt had written the note to evict her from his life.

She'd spent the next two weeks crying, breaking down without warning as she walked down the street, or as she sat staring at a meal she couldn't bring herself to eat.

Candace, she remembered with a bittersweet pang, had tried to get her to go clubbing in order to get her to forget about Matt.

She'd turned her twin down, but she did get her act together. If Matt didn't think enough of their relationship to try to contact her, to try to make her understand why he'd changed so radically from lover to stranger, then to hell with him. He was dead to her, she resolved. And he'd remained that way.

Until twenty minutes ago.

The adrenaline in her veins kept mounting.

Natalie focused on her driving. Vegas in the daylight wasn't nearly as alluring, as magical and glitzy as it was after dark. Like an aging woman best seen in soft lighting, Vegas's imperfections were all visible in the daylight. Natalie supposed that was why people like her sister didn't like to get up until noon. They lived for the night.

Except that Candace could no longer do that.

The thought brought a fresh, sharp ache with it.

"Damn it, Candy, what a waste," Natalie murmured under her breath.

She pulled up before the Janus casino. One of the three valets currently on duty came to life and made a beeline for her vehicle.

"Welcome to the Janus," the young attendant said cheerfully as he opened her door with a flourish.

"We'll see," she replied solemnly.

As he pulled away with her car, Natalie looked up

at the casino's logo. Janus was the Roman god with two faces, one pointed toward the past, the other facing the future. It struck her as rather ironic, given what she was doing here, seeking out someone from her past in order to get answers so that the future could be settled.

The moment she entered the casino, the Vegas phenomena took hold. It was like stepping into a world where time did not matter or even make an appearance. There was only a sense of "now."

Because in Natalie's experience she'd discovered that bartenders knew the inner workings of any establishment they worked for better than anyone else, she made her way to the first bar she saw within the casino.

The bartender in attendance was a gregarious man in his early forties. He had a quick, sexy smile, which was probably one of the main reasons he'd been hired. His name tag identified him as Kevin.

Moving to her end of the bar, Kevin asked, "What'll it be, pretty lady?"

"Information." She saw a dubious look cross his brow. To counter that, she took out her badge. Granted she wasn't here in an official capacity, but Kevin didn't need to know that. "Were you on duty last night?"

Kevin began to wipe the gleaming black surface of the bar. "You mean during the gala?"

"Yes."

The smile gracing his lips was a satisfied one. Last night had obviously been profitable for him, she judged. "I caught an extra shift."

She took out Candace's photograph and carefully placed it on the bar. "Did you happen to see this woman there?"

The bartender glanced at the picture. Mild interest turned to recognition. "You mean Candace Rothchild? Yeah, she was here, loud and brassy as always. But not for long," he added, looking rather disappointed. There was always a circus when Candace was around, Natalie thought. "She and the boss had at it and then he had our head of security escort her out."

She latched onto the first part of his statement. "They argued? About what?"

He shook his head. "Couldn't tell you. Too far away for anything but body language," he confessed.

"And the head of security?" she asked.

"He got her to leave."

She leaned in over the bar. "Tell me about him."

"Don't know much," the bartender admitted. "Just that his name's Matt Shaffer. Boss flew him in from L.A., where he was head of security for Montgomery Enterprises."

There was no avoiding it, she thought darkly. She was going to have to talk to Matt. The thought left her cold. "Do you know where I can find him right now?"

Kevin glanced at his watch. "He should be in his office. On the second floor, toward the rear." He gave her the numbers of the rooms where the monitors that kept watch over the casino guests as they tried their luck against the house were located.

Taking out a twenty, she placed it on the bar. "Thanks for your help."

Kevin slipped the bill into his vest pocket. "Any time, lovely lady," he called after her. "Any time."

She debated going up the stairs, then decided on the elevator. The car that took her up to the second floor was empty. Natalie stepped out of the elevator, looked around to get her bearings and then walked toward the rear of the floor.

"Into the Valley of Death rode the six hundred," she silently recited, digging deep for a line from a poem by Tennyson. Wrapping her hand around a brass handle, she opened one of the glass doors and walked in.

The woman whose desk was closest to the door looked up. "You can't come in here. This is a restricted area."

Natalie already had her ID in her hand and held it up. "I'm looking for Matt Shaffer," she told the woman.

God, even saying his name made her mouth go dry. She was supposed to be over him, to have moved on with her life. What happened?

The woman began to answer her. "He's—"

"Right here."

The deep voice came from behind her. Natalie felt every single nerve ending go on tactical alert at the same moment that all the hairs at the back of her neck stood up. Eight years had passed, but she would have recognized his voice anywhere.

* * * * *

Why did Matt Shaffer leave heiress-turned-cop
Natalie Rothchild?
What does he know about the death of
Natalie's twin sister?
Come and meet these two reunited lovers
and learn the secrets of the Rothchild family in
THE HEIRESS'S 2-WEEK AFFAIR
by USA TODAY bestselling author
Marie Ferrarella.
The first book in Silhouette® Romantic Suspense's
wildly romantic new continuity,
LOVE IN 60 SECONDS!
Available April 2009.

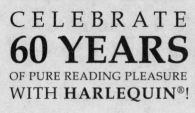

CELEBRATE
60 YEARS
OF PURE READING PLEASURE
WITH **HARLEQUIN®**!

Look for Silhouette®
Romantic Suspense in April!

Love In 60 Seconds

Bright lights. Big city. Hearts in overdrive.

Silhouette® Romantic Suspense is celebrating Harlequin's 60th Anniversary with six stories that promise to bring readers the glitz of Las Vegas, the danger of revenge, the mystery of a missing diamond, and family scandals.

Look for the first title, *The Heiress's 2-Week Affair* by *USA TODAY* bestselling author Marie Ferrarella, on sale in April!

You're invited to join our Tell Harlequin Reader Panel!

By joining our new reader panel you will:

- Receive Harlequin® books—they are FREE and yours to keep with no obligation to purchase anything!
- Participate in fun online surveys
- Exchange opinions and ideas with women just like you
- Have a say in our new book ideas and help us publish the best in women's fiction

In addition, you will have a chance to win great prizes and receive special gifts! See Web site for details. Some conditions apply. Space is limited.

To join, visit us at
www.TellHarlequin.com.

From *New York Times* bestselling author

Gena Showalter

Enter a mythical world
of dragons, demons and nymphs...
Enter a world of dark seduction
and powerful magic...
Enter Atlantis...

Catch these thrilling tales in a bookstore near you!

THE NYMPH KING • Available now!

HEART OF THE DRAGON • Available January 2009

JEWEL OF ATLANTIS • Available February 2009

THE VAMPIRE'S BRIDE • Available March 2009

"Lots of danger and sexy passion give lucky readers a
spicy taste of adventure and romance."
—*Romantic Times BOOKreviews*
on *Heart of the Dragon*

HQN™
We *are* romance™

www.HQNBooks.com   PHGSAT2009

The Inside Romance newsletter has a NEW look for the new year!

Same great content, brand-new look!

The Inside Romance newsletter is a FREE quarterly newsletter highlighting our upcoming series releases and promotions!

Click on the Inside Romance link on the front page of **www.eHarlequin.com** or e-mail us at insideromance@harlequin.ca to sign up to receive your FREE newsletter today!

You can also subscribe by writing to us at: HARLEQUIN BOOKS Attention: Customer Service Department P.O. Box 9057, Buffalo, NY 14269-9057

Please allow 4-6 weeks for delivery of the first issue by mail.

REQUEST YOUR FREE BOOKS!

2 FREE NOVELS PLUS 2 FREE GIFTS!

Silhouette®

nocturne™

Dramatic and Sensual Tales of Paranormal Romance.

YES! Please send me 2 FREE Silhouette® Nocturne™ novels and my 2 FREE gifts (gifts are worth about $10). After receiving them, if I don't wish to receive any more books, I can return the shipping statement marked "cancel." If I don't cancel, I will receive 4 brand-new novels every other month and be billed just $4.47 per book in the U.S. or $4.99 per book in Canada, plus 25¢ shipping and handling per book plus applicable taxes, if any*. That's a savings of about 15% off the cover price! I understand that accepting the 2 free books and gifts places me under no obligation to buy anything. I can always return a shipment and cancel at any time. Even if I never buy another book from Silhouette, the two free books and gifts are mine to keep forever.

238 SDN ELS4   338 SDN ELXG

Name _____ (PLEASE PRINT) _____

Address _____ Apt. # _____

City _____ State/Prov. _____ Zip/Postal Code _____

Signature (if under 18, a parent or guardian must sign) _____

Mail to the **Silhouette Reader Service:**
IN U.S.A.: P.O. Box 1867, Buffalo, NY 14240-1867
IN CANADA: P.O. Box 609, Fort Erie, Ontario L2A 5X3

Not valid to current subscribers of Silhouette Nocturne books.

Want to try two free books from another line?
Call 1-800-873-8635 or visit www.morefreebooks.com.

* Terms and prices subject to change without notice. N.Y. residents add applicable sales tax. Canadian residents will be charged applicable provincial taxes and GST. Offer not valid in Quebec. This offer is limited to one order per household. All orders subject to approval. Credit or debit balances in a customer's account(s) may be offset by any other outstanding balance owed by or to the customer. Please allow 4 to 6 weeks for delivery. Offer available while quantities last.

Your Privacy: Silhouette is committed to protecting your privacy. Our Privacy Policy is available online at www.eHarlequin.com or upon request from the Reader Service. From time to time we make our lists of customers available to reputable third parties who may have a product or service of interest to you. If you would prefer we not share your name and address, please check here. ☐

SN08R